THE GRANNY PROJECT

ANNE FINE

Resource Material
Linda le Versha

Series Consultant
Cecily O'Neill

CollinsEducational
An imprint of HarperCollins*Publishers*

Copyright © Playscript 1986 Anne Fine. Further material Linda le Versha

Originally published as a novel by
Methuen Childrens Book Ltd

First published 1980, reprinted 1987 (twice), 1988, 1990, 1991, 1992, 1993, 1994
Reprinted 1995, 1996, 1998, 1999, 2000, 2001, 2002, 2003

ISBN 000 330234 2

www.**Collins**Education.com

On-line Support for Schools and Colleges

Acknowledgements
The following permissions to reproduce material
are gratefully acknowledged: *The Granny Book*
by Colin Hawkins, Grafton Books, page 52;
British Rail poster – J. Walter Thompson
and Pat Phoenix, page 56; Laurie Lee
extract, The Hogarth Press, pages 57–59;
Bill from *Poems and Family Album*, London
Magazine Editions, pages 63–64; Dylan Thomas
extract, JM Dent & Sons Ltd, pages 63–64;
Gorky extract © Ronald Wilds (translator),
Penguin, page 64; from *Collected Poems by
Frances Cornford*, Century Hutchinson Ltd, page
65; Jenny Joseph, page 66; from *Ageing Today
and Tomorrow*, Age Concern, Mitcham, Surrey,
pages 70 and 73–75.

Design by The Pinpoint Design Company

Typeset by Hope Services, Abingdon.
Printed and bound in China by Imago

CONTENTS

THE CHARACTERS

IVAN   Fourteen, serious and uncompromising. He is in the same school class as his sister —

SOPHIE   Nearly a year younger, and the brains of the family.

TANYA   Ten, sharp-tongued and impatient. She takes her frustration at being younger than Ivan and Sophie out on —

NICHOLAS   Nine. Solemn and innocent; a bit of a day-dreamer.

HENRY HARRIS   The children's father. Forty-two, tired, balding and occasionally dispirited. He teaches languages at the school Ivan and Sophie attend. He is married to —

NATASHA HARRIS   The children's mother. Thirty-six, she is Russian by birth and upbringing, and fiery and tense by nature. She can never work out quite how she ended up trapped in a 'foreign' city suburb with four 'foreign' children and an old lady to care for.

THE DOCTOR   Young and inexperienced. He takes refuge in long medical words.

THE GRANNY PROJECT

ACT I

The play takes place in a large, untidy family kitchen and living area. On one side, stools surround a table in front of the oven, sink and fridge. On the other, two tatty armchairs and a few floor cushions are grouped around a television. There are several doors off. The table is set for four, with sausages and mashed potatoes already cooling on the plates.
Nicholas comes in, eyeing one of the closed doors uneasily. He hushes the audience chatter with a damping down gesture of two spread hands.

NICHOLAS Sssh. **Sssh!** You'll have to be quiet, all of you. It's very important. My gran's in there, behind that door, and she needs absolute quiet. She's busy. She's dying. For all I know, she could be dead already. *He takes a plastic toy soldier off the table and starts twisting its arms and legs around nervously* It's been going on for a week now, her dying. Everyone's worn out. Mum and Dad especially. They've been taking turns to sit up with her every night since Monday. Dad's got huge bags under his eyes. Mum looks grey. *He puts the toy down and faces the audience squarely* It's all my brother Ivan's fault. Well, Tanya, — she's my sister — she says it's all his fault., But Tanya's always saying spiteful things. Sophie — she's my other sister — she tries to shut Tanya up, but . . . oh, this is hopeless. This is no way to explain. I'll have to go right back to the beginning and tell you how it happened from the very start, weeks and weeks ago, the day the doctor first came round to our house to fill in the forms.

Henry, Natasha, Ivan, Sophie, Tanya and the Doctor come in. The children take their places at the table and start eating silently but very fast. Henry hunches gloomily on one of the chairs. Natasha leans against a door with a contemptuous look on her face. The Doctor sits upright, filling in his long form.

NICHOLAS *taking his place at the table* There we all were, minding our own business, politely eating our supper.

Ivan suddenly spins a sausage off his plate onto the floor and reaches down with a fork to stab it.

NATASHA No need to kill your food. It's already dead.

Ivan spits a little out onto the side of his plate.

NATASHA Nor is it poisoned! And so you needn't spit it on the plate.

IVAN That's gristle, that is!

NATASHA Tsssk!

DOCTOR *filling in the form* Osteoarthritis. Metacarpophalangeal joint involvement leading to characteristic volar subluxation and ulnar deviation of the phalanges . . .

HENRY What?

SOPHIE He says Granny's fingers are bent.

HENRY Ah.

DOCTOR Degenerative changes in the cochlea . . .

SOPHIE And she's going deaf.

HENRY Right.

DOCTOR Impairment of brain tissue function with concomitant deterioration of cognitive functioning . . .

NATASHA And stupid, too.

HENRY Natasha!

NATASHA Tssk!

SOPHIE She's still smart enough to get to the newspaper every morning before anyone else.

NATASHA What's in a newspaper to interest you?

SOPHIE Stuff. Stuff for Projects. Any old stuff.

IVAN Everything interests me and Sophie now we do Social

Science — Crime, Violence, Police Corruption, Race Relations, Consumer Protection, Suicide Rates, Sex Statistics . . .

NATASHA Tssk! Projects! Pah! Such a school. For all your father teaches there, I'll take you out of it! **Projects!**

DOCTOR There's no specific ambulatory problem, I take it.

NATASHA The lazy old woman can still walk, yes, if she is truly hungry.

SOPHIE More of a shuffle, really.

HENRY Well, that's because she stole my bedroom slippers. They're several sizes too large for her feet.

DOCTOR Her dietary intake?

NATASHA The woman can eat **anything**!

IVAN She ate the leaves off Sophie's geranium last week. And Nicholas and Tanya caught her chewing feathers this morning.

NATASHA You did? How many?

NICHOLAS Hardly any.

TANYA Tons and tons.

NATASHA See! Stupid and greedy, that is what she is!

HENRY Natasha! Please!

NATASHA *muttering* And she should know the **cost** of pillows.

HENRY Sssh.

NATASHA Tsssk, yourself, Henry Harris! She is not **my** mother!

DOCTOR *folding up the forms and rising* One further manifestation, should we seek it, of the proven versatility of the human gastro-intestinal tract.

NATASHA Just what I said. The woman can eat anything.

DOCTOR I'll see these forms get to the right place. But since there's no immediate problem — **Natasha** *glares at him horribly* Since Mrs Harris isn't actually ill at the moment, results may not be immediate.

IVAN What does he mean? Results? What's going on? Are you two thinking of putting Granny into a Home?

NATASHA Thinking is finished. It is decided.

3

IVAN Dad? **Dad?**

HENRY *clearing his throat in an embarrassed fashion* Your mother and I are finding Granny an enormous strain . . .

NICHOLAS You're never sending Granny **away?**

HENRY Nothing's decided. Nothing for you to worry about. Let's wait and see.

NATASHA *ushering out the doctor* Шипа в мешке не утаишь. [Shipa vmiéskay nye ootáish]

IVAN What?

SOPHIE What did she say?

TANYA What was that?

NICHOLAS What did she just say?

HENRY Nothing.

CHILDREN **Dad!**

HENRY It's only one of her old Russian proverbs.

SOPHIE We know that, Dad. But what does it **mean?**

HENRY It means. . .*He hangs his head in shame* It means you can't hide sharp steel spikes in soft cloth bags.

*Henry goes out after the **Doctor** and **Natasha**.*

SOPHIE *sarcastically* Terrific.

TANYA Lovely.

IVAN Really caring.

NICHOLAS I think it's horrible. Horrible.

*A pause. They are all sunk in thought. Then **Ivan** claps his hands.*

IVAN Meeting! Meeting! Fall in. Take your places.

They quickly form a practised semicircle, and sit down.

IVAN Ready?

ALL Ready.

IVAN Good. Right. First thing. Do we care?

ALL Yes, we do.

IVAN Good. Right. Next thing. Can we stop them?

ALL Yes, we can.

IVAN Good. Right. Last thing. How?

Silence.

TANYA I could have some of my tantrums. Or my nightmares. My tantrums and nightmares really get on their nerves.

NICHOLAS They really get on mine as well. I vote against that.

IVAN How about a strike? No fetching in the coal, no washing-up, no going down to the shops, till they back down.

NICHOLAS They're tougher than we are. They practically remember the **war**. We'll freeze and starve and live in even more of a mess than we do now, and they'll still win. I vote against that.

IVAN Do you have any brilliant ideas of your own?

NICHOLAS Send them to Coventry. Don't say a word to either until they change their minds.

IVAN You must be mad. They'd simply be grateful for all the peace and quiet. They've often said as much. Sophie, you're supposed to be the brains here. Sophie?

Sophie is sunk in thought. Light dawns and she lifts her head.

SOPHIE I've got it!

ALL What?

SOPHIE This Project that was set for homework last week...

IVAN The one for Social Science? The one that counts for half a term's marks?

SOPHIE That's the one. You and me, Ivan, we'll team up for it. We'll work together on a Joint Project, double the length.

IVAN On what?

SOPHIE On ageing people in the community.

Ivan begins to grin. Tanya and Nicholas look blank.

SOPHIE We'll get all the statistics and stuff from newspapers and reference books. That won't take long. But half the Project, a good half of it, will be a vivid and uncensored description —

5

IVAN Of one particular family!

SOPHIE A family with a real old person living in it.

IVAN *pointing to Granny's door* **Her**!

NICHOLAS Who? **Granny**?

IVAN That's right. Our own Granny.

TANYA *acting it out* A little bit doddery on her old pins.

IVAN *imitating* All wrinkly, with fluffy white hair sticking out in every direction.

SOPHIE Tottering about shedding pre-war hatpins.

NICHOLAS I stepped on one yesterday. Didn't half hurt.

TANYA Keeps getting everyone mixed up with everyone else.

IVAN Calls me Henry.

SOPHIE Calls me Natasha.

NICHOLAS Called me Uncle Percy all day yesterday.

TANYA All in all, more than a little bit gaga.

SOPHIE A real old person. A real school Project on a real old person in a real family. We'll get down everything.

IVAN Absolutely everything.

TANYA Everything they say.

NICHOLAS Everything they do.

IVAN Whenever she gets up in the middle of the night and goes round next door in her feather hat and nightie to tell the Hanleys she's come for afternoon tea.

SOPHIE Whenever Dad opens an electricity bill and has a fit to see what it costs to keep her fire on all day and night.

NICHOLAS Whenever Mum curses and spits and says we haven't had a proper holiday for nine whole years, not even a weekend.

TANYA Whenever Dad says if she won't die off naturally, he'll just have to bloody well poison her.

ALL It all goes down in the Granny Project!

IVAN That'll stop them. Settle their nonsense once and for all!

*All look triumphant except **Nicholas**, who looks puzzled.*

6

NICHOLAS Why?

IVAN I beg your pardon?

NICHOLAS Why? Why will that stop them? Why will you and Sophie handing in a Project on Granny at school stop Mum and Dad putting her into a Home?

IVAN It's **obvious**, Nicholas. Dad teaches there. He has colleagues and friends. If we wrote down the half of what goes on in this house and gave it in, the sordid details would get round the staffroom in a flash.

SOPHIE You know what it's like in staffrooms, don't you? You've seen them, haven't you, all sitting around, slurping their fourth cup of coffee.

IVAN Grousing about their pay and conditions.

SOPHIE So busy grumbling they don't even hear the bell ring.

IVAN No one could read a Project like this one —

SOPHIE Dynamite. Pure dynamite!

IVAN And keep it quiet. No chance.

SOPHIE And Dad's not daft. We'll leave the Project lying around as soon as it's finished.

NICHOLAS You can't! He'll read it! He always does! He can't see a schoolbook lying about without having a good snoop.

TANYA That's the teacher in him. It's in the bones.

IVAN His having a good snoop is the whole **point** of it, Nicholas. The minute he reads it he'll realise that the day our Project is handed in at school is the day his reputation is ruined.

TANYA He'll never lift his head in the staffroom again!

NICHOLAS That's **horrible**, that is. That's dirty, disgusting blackmail!

IVAN Listen, Nicholas. Do you want to see Granny parcelled off to some Old People's Home, or don't you? You can't have it both ways. You can't make omelettes without breaking eggs. Those two out there mean business. They've had enough. Nine years she's been here, getting steadily worse. They want her out before they're too old to enjoy themselves.

But we think she should stay. She's old and feeble and confused. She shouldn't be with strangers. This is her home.

SOPHIE   It's true, Nicholas. They'll send her off to some big strange house that smells of disinfectant all over, and she'll be shoved in a room with three other ancient biddies she's never been introduced to.

IVAN   And if she wanders about getting in everyone's way, like she does here, they'll give her pills to make her so woozy she'll stay in bed.

TANYA   And no one will have time to stop and talk to her, like Mum and Dad do whenever they can stand it.

SOPHIE   We'll be too busy to visit, except at weekends.

TANYA   And in the end, she'll just give up and **die**.

IVAN   And it will be our fault, because we didn't act on our principles and make a stand at the beginning.

TANYA   Because little baby Nicholas was too wet for a teensy bit of blackmail!

NICHOLAS   *dubiously*   Maybe you're right. . .

TANYA   Of **course** we're right.

SOPHIE   Oh, Nicholas, don't fret about it. I know that blackmail isn't very nice, but, after all, it is all in a good cause.

IVAN   A **very** good cause.

NICHOLAS   Well . . . If you all say so . . . I suppose you must be right . . .

IVAN   Oh, well done, Nicholas! I knew you'd see sense!

SOPHIE   Good old Nicholas.

TANYA   About time, too!

*As **Nicholas** begins to speak, the others drift to the back of the room and start dividing pads and pens, to take notes.*

NICHOLAS   So that's how the Granny Project got started. Sophie gave everyone a pad and pen, and off we went, watching and taking notes on anything at all to do with Granny. I say watching, but it was really more like spying. And very easy spying, too, since Mum and Dad weren't on the look-out. They were both far too frazzled with running the house, and bringing in the money, and serving up meals,

8

and all that stuff, on top of looking after Granny night and day. They didn't even notice the four of us, sitting so innocently in corners apparently doing our homework. And some of it was really good fun, especially at the start. There was the time she sent Dad out at midnight to buy a floral wreath for Mr Hanley, who isn't even dead. And the time Dad took a bit out of the back of her telly and told her there was a strike on all four channels, just so she'd go to bed and he could watch the snooker in peace and quiet.

SOPHIE *lifting her head* And don't forget the time she said to me: 'You're very bossy. Are you one of that Natasha's children? Or are you one of Henry's?'

NICHOLAS And the night he came back from taking her to vote.

IVAN The night of the General Election.

TANYA God, that was funny.

NICHOLAS He was **furious** when she insisted on going.

SOPHIE 'Exercising her democratic right and duty'. That's what she called it. And she **made** him take her.

TANYA And what a mood he was in when they came back!

Natasha comes in and sits reading the paper. Tanya and Nicholas sit at the table gluing a model. Sophie is reading. Henry enters through Granny's door, backwards, his coat on.

HENRY Yes, mum. Yes, mum. Yes, the moment we know who's won the election, I'll let you know. Mum, my coat's wet through. I'll have to take it off. I'll be back in a moment. *He shuts the door and turns on the family* Right! Which one of you was it? Confess! Which one of you was daft enough to mention to her that this was an Election night? Hmmm?

TANYA *coldly* There's a large sign gone up outside her window. It says: **To the Polling Station**.

HENRY That's no excuse! Voting! At her age! Ridiculous! She must have lost her grasp on the subtleties of British politics shortly before the Suez Crisis! What difference does it make to **her** what lot gets in? Pensioners always do all right. You see them hobbling out of the post offices with their fists full of tenners. What does it matter to them which party's in power? *He turns on Sophie* And what were **you** doing creeping along behind, may I enquire?

SOPHIE *innocently* I was just watching democracy in action. You never know when you'll be covering it in some Project.

NATASHA Tsssk! Projects! Pah!

HENRY The embarrassment of escorting her there in her carpet slippers!

SOPHIE I'm sure the polling officers didn't mind.

HENRY Mind? **Mind?** I was practically arrested! They thought I'd dragged her there against her will to vote for the party I support.

SOPHIE That wasn't your fault. That was because she asked you in such a loud voice: 'Henry, dear. Where shall I put my little cross?'

HENRY The **shame** of it.

SOPHIE I thought the worst was when her bloomers fell down.

HENRY Oh, God! Her bloomers! I could have **died!**

IVAN Surely a vote for Socialism is worth a pair of fallen knickers.

TANYA She didn't vote for Socialism.

SOPHIE Sssh, Tanya! Ssssh!

HENRY What's that? Didn't vote for our woman? Who the hell did she vote for then? Gay Punk?

TANYA She didn't vote for anyone.

HENRY What do you know about it? You weren't even there. I saw her putting her cross onto the paper.

TANYA And so did Sophie. And Sophie says she put her cross exactly in between the top two candidates.

HENRY What? Spoiled her vote?

SOPHIE She didn't have her spectacles on.

HENRY After all that effort! All that trouble! The humiliation! Wasted her vote!

IVAN It looks like it.

HENRY I'll kill her. I will kill her. I will. It's senile old folk like her who don't know which way up a ballot paper goes that bring in landslide victories for this bloody lot, time and again.

NATASHA Lucky to be where voting counts, and have more than one candidate to vote for.

HENRY I don't know how you've got the nerve to say that, Natasha. You didn't vote. You only sat here reading the paper. I was the one who went out in the cold and wet, and took her with me. At a **snail's** pace, I might add. We both got sodden wet. And all that for a wasted vote!

NATASHA Where I come from, all votes are wasted votes. And anyway, изменеие власти, удовлетворение дураков [Ismenénya vlásti oodavletvarénye dúrakov.]

IVAN What?

SOPHIE What did she say?

TANYA What was that?

NICHOLAS What?

HENRY She said: A change of rulers is the satisfaction of fools. *The door bell rings* Who's that?

NATASHA *rising* The Doctor. *She makes for the door* Cheer up, my darling. There is always hope. Молодои врач, жолмистое кладбище [Maladoy vrach, hulmistoye kladbishe.]

HENRY *following her out, but popping his head back round the door* She said: Young doctor, humpy churchyard.

NICHOLAS That isn't very nice at all.

SOPHIE *standing up and reading from her notes* An old person's feet can swell so much from sitting all day that simply crushing them into outdoor shoes can prove impossible. Walking is difficult, even with help, especially in the dark and wet. It's hard to see without your spectacles, and hard to remember your spectacles when you are old. So even a simple thing like casting her vote in a General Election put an enormous strain upon Old Granny Harris.

IVAN And other members of the family.

SOPHIE *slowly, writing it in* And–other–members–of– the – family.

*The **Doctor**, **Natasha** and **Henry** come out of Granny's room.*

DOCTOR What we have here is simply lumbar osteoarthritis compressing nerve roots, with this resultant paresthesia.

11

HENRY   What's paresthesia?

DOCTOR   Jumpy legs.

HENRY   I beg your pardon?

DOCTOR   Jumpy legs.

HENRY   Oh, so it's jumpy legs she's got now, is it?

NATASHA   You've got them, too. You'll no doubt go the way your mother's gone. This paresthesia is, no doubt, some Harris family curse.

HENRY   Thank you, Natasha.

DOCTOR   It's not your problem for much longer, anyway. The whole thing should be off your hands within a week. They'll let you know what she's to bring, and what time you're to take her in.

Henry follows him out. The children look reproachfully at Natasha.

NATASHA   Don't look at me like that! Don't you dare! Only when you have laid me and your father kindly and safely in **our** graves may you look at me as you do now. Only then!

She slams out of the room.

TANYA   Did you hear that? Within a week. We haven't time to wait any longer.

IVAN   We have enough. Sophie's put most of it together. It's just about ready.

*Sophie shuffles papers together into a folder entitled: **The Granny Project**.*

NICHOLAS   Have you got my list of the the times Natasha had to wash extra sheets this week?

TANYA   Did you get my description of when she spilled her tea three times in a row?

IVAN   Don't leave out my chart of how many times on average per evening she calls Henry to change her television channel.

SOPHIE   It's all here. All together. Behind the bit where Dad says the only thing she's good for is sitting by the window frightening off Avon Ladies.

IVAN   Right, Sophie. Lay it down on the table.

NICHOLAS Are you **sure** this is the best thing to do?

SOPHIE *suddenly dubious* It is strong stuff, Ivan. Some of the things in here would sound simply dreadful to an outsider.

TANYA There's going to be one hell of a row.

SOPHIE I feel disloyal, like a family traitor.

NICHOLAS Blackmail's disgusting. I feel awful.

TANYA It's going to get us into terrible trouble.

IVAN Listen, you lot, we have a purpose we believe in.

SOPHIE The ends don't justify the means.

IVAN You have to keep your feelings **out** of this.

SOPHIE You sound like a terrorist, or a hijacker.

IVAN They get things done.

SOPHIE What sort of things? Getting people killed?

IVAN Revolutions, for one thing. The people who dissolve into puddles of tears about starving peasants might write out cheques, but it's revolutionaries who get the peasants back their own land!

SOPHIE And get thousands killed while they're about it!

IVAN Dead of wounds, dead of hunger. What's the difference?

SOPHIE You've got no feelings at all, have you?

IVAN Better than not being able to think straight.

SOPHIE I'd rather not think straight if it ends up as crooked as this.

IVAN At least I have a plan, and one that will work.

SOPHIE Oh sure! Like kidnapping your enemy's children. Or ripping out people's fingernails to get the information you want.

NICHOLAS *horrified* People don't really do that, do they?

SOPHIE Oh, yes. They do. People with noble ideals and no real feelings. People like Ivan here.

*Ivan slaps **Sophie**'s face. **Sophie** slaps **Ivan** back. They stare at one another.*

SOPHIE *with ice in her voice* That's it. I'm having nothing more to do with this. Cross my name off that folder.

13

Ivan scratches out her name.

NICHOLAS   I don't want to be part of this, either.

TANYA   Nor me.

Ivan picks up the folder.

IVAN   I hope you'll all feel just as sanctimonious when Granny's carted off to that Home!

He gives one last look at the folder, then slams it down on the table and rushes out. The others look at one another, appalled. **Nicholas** *bursts into tears.* **Sophie** *puts her arm round him and leads him out.* **Tanya** *follows.* **Henry,** *who wanders in holding a coffee cup, steps aside to let them pass. He looks after them curiously, then shrugs. He catches sight of the folder, picks it up and rifles through casually. Something engages his attention. He peers more closely. He turns the pages more slowly, and with a frown that deepens into a look of sheer fury. He reads the name on the cover. Then, throwing back his head, he bellows:*

HENRY   IVAN! **IVAN!**

ACT II

*Henry is standing behind the kitchen table on which the
Granny Project lies like a trial exhibit. **Ivan** is standing in
front.*

HENRY This thing here. This — Granny Project. Well . . . ?

IVAN Yes?

HENRY **I'm** asking **you!**

IVAN Well, I was going to hand it in on Monday.

HENRY Is it a joke?

IVAN No. Not a joke.

HENRY Who chose this topic?

IVAN It was Sophie's idea at the very start.

HENRY I don't see Sophie's name on this.

IVAN Sophie dropped out.

HENRY Thought better of it, you mean?

IVAN Changed her mind, yes.

HENRY And so it's all yours now. And what's it for?

IVAN Well, it's for Social Science homework, in one
sense . . .

HENRY And in another . . . ?

IVAN I suppose, in another, you could say that it was
blackmail.

HENRY Blackmail?

IVAN Blackmail. To stop you putting Granny into that
Home.

15

HENRY   We keep your Granny here, or you hand this in at school.

IVAN   That's right.

HENRY   I see. Tell me, this thing, this vicious and disloyal document, this hurtful and insensitive catalogue of eavesdroppings — you don't feel this to be dishonourable?

IVAN   I **feel** it is, yes. But I don't **think** it is. With Sophie, the feelings took over. That's why she dropped out in the end. I reconsidered then. Of course I did. But still I thought that I was right, so I kept going.

HENRY   Ivan, it makes me ill to think a son of mine could act like this. That he could think this thing through in such a cold, inhuman fashion. You carry on this way and God knows what a barbarous mess you'll make of your life. You live in this house. You know what a strain it's been looking after my mother. Where's your sympathy, your understanding, your warmth? If you can act this way in your own family, where do you think you will end up?

IVAN   Sophie thinks I'll become a revolutionary.

HENRY   Christ, Ivan! What a terrible waste!

IVAN   I don't see why.

HENRY   You know what happens to revolutionaries. They don't live long. They die or rot alive in jails. You can't **do** anything in prison, you know. That's the whole point of them. So if you want to change things, make things better, you have to stay out here with the rest of us.

IVAN   That's what I'm doing, isn't it? I'm changing something now. Changing your mind about sending Granny into that Home. That's why I wrote the Granny Project. I worked very hard, too. I had a purpose, and I still believe in it. You're hurt and angry, I know that; but I knew from the start that you would be. I took that into account.

HENRY   You're not a grown up revolutionary yet, you know. And I'm still your father. I could just burn this folder.

IVAN   I'm not playing games, Dad. I have copies.

HENRY   Ivan, I'm coming very close indeed to hitting you — **hard**.

IVAN   That isn't going to help.

HENRY   I would feel better.

16

IVAN Feelings, again.

HENRY Get out! Get out of here! **Get out!**

Hastily, **Ivan** *leaves.* **Henry** *puts his head in his hands.*
Natasha *comes in.*

HENRY That son of yours is an absolute monster. Do you
know what he's up to? He's written about everything that's
happened in this house to do with my mother — everything!
Down to the most private things! And now he's threatening
to hand it in at school as a Project, unless we change our
minds about putting her in a Home. You said that he'd
seemed quiet and busy and absorbed in his work recently.
Well, *tapping the Granny Project* this is what he's been
quiet and busy and absorbed in — blackmail! Sheer blackmail!

NATASHA Ivan was single-minded from the womb.

HENRY Unfeeling is what I call it.

NATASHA He will go far.

HENRY Go far? **Go far?** He'll end up some cold and
merciless terrorist, leaving his wife and children to go off
and kill perfect strangers for some lofty principles.
Liquidating all those with different priorities, hurling his
bombs, dying from bullets or starving himself to death in
some cell.

NATASHA There are all sorts of ways of fighting battles.

HENRY You think he's **right**?

NATASHA I'm not sure that he's wrong.

HENRY You know what happened to your own country's
revolution?

NATASHA I also know about the way things were before for
most of the people. Чем дальше в лес, тем больше дров.
[Chem dalshay vooliéss, tyem bolshay drov.]

HENRY The further into the woods you go, the more trees
there are. What kind of proverb is **that**, for God's sake?

NATASHA What kind of parents are we, to be outwitted by
our own blood and bone?

HENRY Oh, don't remind me! A blackmailer in my own
family! My own son. My first born. It chills my blood.

NATASHA You are quite right. Of all the crimes to choose!

He should be something useful, like a poisoner, and practise on his Granny.

HENRY   I could just beat him up. I would enjoy that.

NATASHA   You hold him. I will beat him up.

HENRY   We could throw him out of the house. He's forfeited all rights to be a member of this family. How old is he, and what's the law? Is Ivan old enough to be thrown out?

NATASHA   Любовь не картошка, не выбросишь в окошко. (Loobov nye cartóshka, nye víbrosish vakóshka.]

HENRY   *translating incredulously* Love is not a potato: you cannot throw it out of the window. I never heard that one before.

NATASHA   I never had sad cause to say it before. Listen, my darling, I have a plan.

She whispers in his ear. A look of amazement and delight comes over his face.

NATASHA   Now go and tell him we agree to his terms. I'll phone the Home and tell them that Mrs Harris stays here. You take the Granny Project from him, and all his copies, and burn them, every scrap.

HENRY   I'll burn them, don't you worry. I'll even poke the bloody ashes to pieces.

Henry strides out and Natasha picks up the phone. While she is making the call, Sophie, Tanya and Nicholas come in and start setting the table for supper. Outside, Henry can be heard whistling.

TANYA   Dad's very cheerful out there in the garden.

NICHOLAS   He's got a bonfire going. He's burning something.

Ivan comes in just as Natasha replaces the receiver.

IVAN   Was that the phone call to the Old People's Home?

NATASHA   Indeed it was.

IVAN   You've cancelled Granny.

NATASHA   Granny is cancelled, yes.

IVAN   *smugly* That's that, then. That's all settled.

SOPHIE   What's settled?

TANYA What's going on?

NICHOLAS What?

NATASHA Your grandmother is staying here. And I must say, it is a comfort to your father and me that Ivan cares for his Granny so dearly. Some might have thought the Granny Project a nasty piece of blackmail; but Henry and I prefer to think it was our own dear first born's only way of letting us know how very strongly he feels about his beloved Granny's well-being.

She gives him a radiant smile. He looks embarrassed and uneasy.

NATASHA Ivan has made his own position entirely clear. His Granny must be cared for in this house. Right?

IVAN *suspicious* Right.

NATASHA Fine. Very well. It is agreed. The Granny Project has been burned. Granny stays here. And Ivan himself will do all the caring.

SOPHIE What?

TANYA Ivan?

NICHOLAS By **himself**?

IVAN **Me**?

NATASHA You.

IVAN What do you mean, exactly — do all the caring?

NATASHA *airily* Oh, you know. You've seen your father and me do it for nine years. Taking trays in and out ten times a day. Fetching and carrying. Bed changing. Laundering. Medicine giving. Sewing on buttons. Fetching her pension. Buying her peppermints. Changing her television channel. Filling her hot water bottles. Sitting with her for hours. Keeping her room warm. Switching on her lamps when it gets dark and switching them off again when she falls asleep. Tuning her radio. Finding her spectacles. Picking up her book. Closing her window. Opening her window. Drawing her curtains. Writing her few remaining Christmas cards. Consoling her when her friends die. Reminding her to eat . . . Why are you staring at me? Have I **missed** something?

IVAN I have to do all that? By myself?

NATASHA Do as you please. Share it between the four of you or do it yourself. You care so much. You can arrange it.

SOPHIE What about you and Dad?

NATASHA We will take over your jobs, of course.

NICHOLAS Our jobs? What jobs?

NATASHA Oh, you know. Popping in to see her whenever the other television is blinking. Worrying about her going into a Home. Putting heads round the door to say goodnight, when you remember. I think that sums it up. Have I missed something?

TANYA You're **joking**. You **must** be.

NATASHA *striking her hand on the table* **Not joking. I am not joking**.

SOPHIE But . . .

NATASHA No buts! No buts, no backsliding. The first time I hear a grumble, she goes!

Silence. Then Ivan laughs.

IVAN Blackmail! Checkmate! You win! Congratulations!

Natasha smiles modestly and extends her hand. He leans over and kisses it.

NATASHA *fondly* My blood and bone. You will go far.

They go off, arm in arm. Sophie and Tanya follow, shaking their heads. Nicholas, left alone, turns to the audience:

NICHOLAS So that's what happened. Ivan had blackmailed them, so they trumped him. They meant what they said, too. From that day on, everything changed. You've no idea how different things were in this house. Dad signed on for evening classes in Woodwork, and Mum took up Italian. Three times a week they tarted up and went out dancing. They didn't look like parents at all. They didn't act like them either, when they came back late . . . What about Ivan? Well, that's a bit embarrassing . . . Sophie and Tanya and me, we did **begin** by doing our share. We felt a little guilty. Ivan had fought the battle, **and** failed his Social Science project. He'd nothing to hand in, you see. Sophie managed to cobble something together in a hurry; but Ivan hadn't the time, what with his new responsibilities. Then we began dropping out, one by one. Tanya was pushed for time because of her netball. Sophie spends ages on homework. I did my bit; but then the weather got better and all my friends came round a little earlier. In the end, I'm afraid Ivan got landed with most of it, really . . .

Nicholas stoops to root in his satchel. Tanya comes in through one door, Ivan through another, carrying a box. Sophie follows Ivan in and gives him a friendly clout on the back.

IVAN Careful. Don't jog.

TANYA What's in that box?

IVAN Rock cakes. Miss Higgins said that they were excellent.

SOPHIE Rockier than everyone else's, were they?

IVAN Would you like to try one?

SOPHIE No, thanks. I can't afford to get weighed down tonight. I'm going to paint the backcloth for the school play.

IVAN You? Chosen to help paint the backcloth?

SOPHIE Yes, me. Picasso Harris.

By now, Nicholas has taken a brightly coloured apron from his satchel, and put it on.

IVAN What's that extraordinary thing you're wearing?

NICHOLAS My pinafore. It's finished. It's taken me eight weeks to make.

TANYA Pass it over. Let's see the hem.

NICHOLAS *struggling* I'm stuck in it.

SOPHIE *helping* You've got a knot. If only you'd learn how to tie a proper bow. . .

TANYA Doesn't Nicholas even know how to tie bows?

NICHOLAS Why should I know how to tie bows? I'm not a **girl**

As Sophie ties a bow in place of the knot, Natasha comes in dressed to go dancing.

NATASHA You are all very late from school. I have been waiting.

IVAN Look! Rock cakes! I made them. They're very good indeed. Have one.

21

TANYA I deserve two. I wrote an essay today, three pages long, and Mr Beaver stuck it up on the wall. He said it was to serve as an inspiration to those in the class who had barely started.

NICHOLAS *spinning like a model* My pinafore's finished. What do you think of it? My hemming was so neat, I was allowed to use the sewing machine to finish the band.

SOPHIE Is there anything other than rock cakes to eat? I'm starving, but I can't stay for supper. I have to go back and help paint the backcloth. Only four people were chosen, and I was one of them.

NATASHA *snatching up her coat and pecking each of them on the cheek in turn. To **Ivan**:* Very nice rock cakes, I'm sure. *To **Nicholas**:* Very good pinafore. *To **Tanya**:* I'm very pleased about your essay. *To **Sophie**:* I hope you have a very nice time painting the backcloth. But I am off. I'm very late. Goodbye.

*The door slams after her. Everyone stands in stony silence glaring at the door. Then **Nicholas** struggles furiously out of his pinafore, throws it down, and stamps on it.*

NICHOLAS *imitating his mother* 'Very nice. Very good. Very pleased. Very late. Goodbye.'

SOPHIE Come off it, Nicholas. It's not that bad.

NICHOLAS It is. It **is** that bad.

He snatches up a handful of rock cakes, and hurls them at the door.

SOPHIE Good rock cakes, Ivan. You've got some first-rate ammunition there for your next brilliant family revolution.

TANYA I'm not clearing that mess up. It's Nicholas's fault.

IVAN It's my fault really. I'll clear it up after I've taken Granny's tea tray in to her. Just please try not to kick it all about.

Sighing, he picks up the tray and goes into Granny's room.

TANYA **She** always gets looked after. I'm starving hungry.

SOPHIE I don't suppose there's anything cooking in the oven . . .

They all sniff. Then they all freeze and sniff again. Looks of sheer horror replace the sniffing.

TANYA What's that **disgusting** smell?

SOPHIE I know what that is.

NICHOLAS So do I.

TANYA It **can't** be. Ivan's supposed to launder all Granny's messy stuff as soon as it happens.

SOPHIE Clearly it's all still rotting in a heap behind that door.

NICHOLAS Ivan's got so behind.

TANYA If he doesn't get a move on, he'll still be at it tomorrow when he should be swimming. He's not been at the pool on time once since he took over caring for Granny. Coach said if he was late just one more time, he's off the team.

SOPHIE Then maybe one of us ought to start on the laundry. I've got to get back into school, but . . .

TANYA Don't look at me! I'm not doing one more extra job for Ivan this week.

NICHOLAS It's for Granny, really.

TANYA You do it, then.

NICHOLAS I can't. I said I'd be down at the playing field by five. It's ten past now.

TANYA Oh, well. It's Ivan's fault. It's Ivan's lookout.

SOPHIE We're out of washing powder anyway. Didn't he get any yesterday?

NICHOLAS No. Mum was late back and he couldn't leave Granny.

TANYA He'd better not forget tomorrow.

NICHOLAS They're going out again tomorrow.

TANYA So why can't he go now?

SOPHIE Because they're both out.

TANYA We're still here, aren't we? Why can't he just run down to the shops and get it now?

SOPHIE Tanya, it's not just the washing powder, you know. We're out of tons of stuff. Her Ovaltine is almost gone. We're out of those tins of rice pudding she eats. She's still waiting for her peppermints. We haven't got this week's Radio Times yet. If he goes down to the shops this evening, he'll be at least an hour, so one of you two will have to stay in.

NICHOLAS   I can't stay in. My friends are waiting.

TANYA   And I was late for netball **last** week, because Ivan took so long down at the shops.

SOPHIE   Well, maybe Mum and Dad will get back soon.

NICHOLAS   They won't be back for hours. They've gone off dancing!

TANYA   Dancing again! They're **always** out dancing!

SOPHIE   It's better than his woodwork evening. I can't **stand** his woodwork evening.   *Imitating*   'Where is my chisel? Where did you put my clamp? Has anyone seen my fretsaw? Who's touched my dowelling rods?' I can't **stand** his woodwork evening, I tell you.

TANYA   It's not as bad as her Italian night. The next time she sails in here at ten o'clock and says 'Molto bene' to my ironing pile, I'm going to strangle her with one of her own stockings.

SOPHIE   I've still got piles of homework to do.

NICHOLAS   Ivan can't even have started his.

TANYA   He must have. What's this folder here?   *She picks it up*   That's Ivan's writing, surely.

SOPHIE   What is that?

TANYA   *opening the folder*   Oh, no!

NICHOLAS   What?

SOPHIE   Let me see.

Tanya hands over the folder. Sophie stares.

SOPHIE   **The Granny Project II, for Social Science, by Ivan Harris, VQ**. Oh, not again! He must be **mad**!

They are gathered around, reading the folder, when **Ivan** *strolls back in.*

SOPHIE   Ivan, what's this?

IVAN   What?

SOPHIE   This. This folder here. This **Granny Project II**. You must be mad to start again.

IVAN   I haven't started again. This is quite different.

24

TANYA How? It's a Granny Project, isn't it?

IVAN It's about Granny, yes. Why shouldn't it be? I have to write another Project for Social Science. She's sitting there. I'm sitting with her. I boil her eggs. She tells me all about her country childhood. It's fair exchange. Some of it's very interesting.

Sophie flicks through. Something catches her eye.

SOPHIE Yuk! Ugh! Ee-**yuk**!

IVAN Is that the bit about eating dead mice to cure the whooping cough?

NICHOLAS They never did that, did they?

IVAN Oh, yes. Her mother told her it was common practice. People would send for the doctor. 'He'll have to come,' they'd say. 'She's eaten up all her dead mouse like a good girl, and still she's no better.'

TANYA Bleh!

NICHOLAS Op, plop, pass the mop!

SOPHIE *leafing through* What's this bit here? Did cobwebs really bind up cuts?

IVAN Granny says cobwebs work much better than Elastoplast.

SOPHIE And ivy leaves soaked in vinegar for corns?

IVAN Everyone had corns. It came from always wearing hand-me-down shoes. They all had chilblains, too.

TANYA Chilblains? I thought it was only old people who got chilblains.

IVAN Granny says anyone who's cold enough for long enough gets chilblains. She says that they were always cold. Sometimes they would be sent to school with baked potatoes to keep their hands warm. But then the school house was as cold as the farm. The fire barely took the chill off a corner of the room. The ink froze in the ink pots. She says you couldn't hear the teacher for all the coughing. She said the coughing went on hour after hour, week after week, all winter. It was like barking, Granny says. And some years they weren't all better till you could step on six daises at once.

NICHOLAS Till you could step on six daises at once?

IVAN Till summer, Granny means. But they were always

covered in chilblains. They had them on their hands and their feet, even their knees and ears. She says you couldn't cram your toes into your boots without crying.

TANYA It sounds quite horrible.

IVAN Some winters it was worse than that. Some winters, they went hungry.

NICHOLAS You mean there wasn't enough food to go round. Like in a famine?

IVAN Well, not exactly famine. But pretty miserable.

SOPHIE *reading from the folder* Old Mrs Harris says that once, when her mother was young and times were very hard indeed, the farm even ran out of acorns to feed the pigs, and grandfather boiled up the cat's drowned kittens, and fed them those instead.

NICHOLAS He didn't!

SOPHIE No!

TANYA I couldn't have stood that.

IVAN They used up everything. Nothing was wasted. They used stale beer for furniture polish, and rubbed it on with a dead rabbit's paw. They used all the plucked hen's feathers in pillows and counterpanes.

SOPHIE Their beds must have been **crawling**.

IVAN They baked the feathers in the oven first, to kill the crawlies.

NICHOLAS Which regulo was that?

TANYA There weren't any regulos then, pea-brain. It was all hot or medium or warm.

NICHOLAS Well, which? Now I can use the sewing machine I wouldn't mind knowing a recipe for home-made pillowcases. Feathers are free and there's always someone's birthday coming along.

IVAN Go and ask Granny.

TANYA You wait for me. I want to know as well. You're not to know more Social Science than me.

*Tanya and **Nicholas** rush into Granny's room*

SOPHIE You've learned an awful lot. I'm almost envious.

IVAN I've enjoyed it — I think. When you're alone with her

26

before the television gets put on and everything's quiet, she gets to ramble on quite a bit. The most amazing things come out — things you would never imagine. Do you know that she can remember what it was like when there were no traffic markings on any of the roads, and how they all laughed to see the first men bending over and painting lines and dashes along the road. And she knows all sorts of things about farming. Like you should never even think of planting your barley until the earth feels warm on your bum.

SOPHIE   Warm on your bum?

IVAN   That's what she said. And she knows funny little farming rhymes, like:

> *Four seeds you have to sow:*
> *One for rook, and one for crow,*
> *One to die, and one to grow.*

And she says farms were all different. At the next one along the valley, the cockerel was separated from the hens every Sunday, for decency's sake. And the farmer's little girl was once beaten just for standing and watching some cow calve. And . . .

NICHOLAS   Ivan! Sophie!

TANYA   You'll have to come!

They run in.

NICHOLAS   Granny's slumped in the chair.

TANYA   She can't sit up straight, and she's breathing funny.

NICHOLAS   Her eyes look weird!

TANYA   I don't think she can see properly.

NICHOLAS   Oh, hurry! Come and help!

IVAN   Quick, Sophie! **Quick!**

They run from the room.

ACT III

Nicholas comes in, hushing the audience just as he did at the very start of the play.

NICHOLAS Sssh. Ssssh! There you all go again, making that awful din. Mind you, it is hard to keep quiet the whole time. We know all about that. Since Granny fell ill, we've had to go pussy-footing round the house remembering not to slam doors, and think twice before we even flush a lavatory. She's not getting any better, either. First that collapse, that gave us all so much of a fright. Then, while she was still weak and poorly from that, she caught a terrible cold off Ivan, and now they're all shaking their heads and saying 'Bronchitis'. The doctor's given her penicillin and all that stuff; but apparently things aren't so simple when you're as old as Granny is. It's different if you're young. All they gave Ivan was a box of tissues.

Ivan comes in wearing a dressing gown and clutching a box of tissues. He blows his nose noisily as Sophie and Tanya come in another door.

TANYA You look disgusting.

IVAN I feel disgusting. I'm not sure why I bothered to come down. I can't face supper.

NICHOLAS You're lucky, then. There isn't any supper to face.

IVAN What's that in the oven?

NICHOLAS That's just my feathers.

TANYA You're never cooking feathers **again**.

28

IVAN   I don't care if he's cooking headlice. I'd just as soon throw up as eat. I'm going back to bed.

He shuffles out, noisily blowing his nose.

SOPHIE   This is ridiculous. We simply can't go on like this. We haven't had a proper supper for days. This house is in chaos. If we don't move now to protect ourselves, we're going to find that every time Ivan has to take a few days off, we're doing all our jobs **and** all of his extra ones **and** looking after both him and Granny while Mum and Dad keep going out dancing. I think it's time things in this household were evened up again.

NICHOLAS   Evened up?

SOPHIE   Fair shares for all — including Mum and Dad.

TANYA   She said no grumbling, or Granny goes.

SOPHIE   More than one way to skin a cat . . . I've got it! Brilliant!

NICHOLAS   What?

SOPHIE   No time to explain. If it's to work, we have to do it straight away, this evening, while Ivan's looking so rotten and ill. I'll need some money.

NICHOLAS   Tanya's got a little.

SOPHIE   What time does that posh delicatessen close?

TANYA   Seven o'clock.

SOPHIE   Quick. Action Stations. No time to lose if we're to get there and back and I'm to brush up on Social Science before supper.

NICHOLAS   Brush up on Social Science?

SOPHIE   You wait and see. All knowledge comes in useful sooner or later. Nicholas, you stay and lay the table. Set it with all the very best stuff they usually keep back for best. Make it look fancy, Nicholas. Absolutely **splendid**. And when Tanya and I walk in, **whatever** we're carrying, **whatever** we say, don't act surprised.

NICHOLAS   Don't act surprised.

SOPHIE   Not at anything.

NICHOLAS   Right.

SOPHIE Quick, Tanya. Run and fetch the money. I'll bring the serving dishes.

*Sophie roots out two huge platters, and follows **Tanya** from the room. Left alone, **Nicholas** delves in odd places and quickly sets the table with a fancy cloth, candlesticks, fresh flowers, a silver cruet, best plates and cutlery. While he is lighting the candles, **Natasha** and **Henry** sail in, arm in arm.*

HENRY Good Lord. Have we come into the wrong kitchen?

NATASHA Oh, Nikki! Darling! There's something special in the oven, yes? *She flings open the oven door. A cloud of feathers flies up in her face* Blast! Hell!

HENRY What's going on?

NICHOLAS Nothing.

NATASHA Nothing? **Nothing**? It is nothing to find my oven filled with filthy foetid bird feathers?

NICHOLAS They're not filthy and foetid. They're nice and clean. And if you hadn't opened the door, they'd have been sterilised in just twenty minutes.

NATASHA *dangerously* What are you up to, little feather-cooker?

NICHOLAS Nothing.

NATASHA Tsssk! В тихом омуте черти водятся. [Fteekom amóotye chertée vadyátsa.]

*Terrified, **Nicholas** hides behind his father.*

HENRY She didn't threaten to kill you, you know. She only said that Devils live in quiet ponds.

NICHOLAS I'm not a quiet pond.

NATASHA Tssk! **Tsssk!**

HENRY Natasha, instead of terrifying the boy, why don't you simply ask him what's going on.

NATASHA *with extreme menace* What's going on, my little feather-cooker?

NICHOLAS We-ell . . .

NATASHA You shake him! He will answer faster!

HENRY Natasha!

NATASHA Tsssk!

NICHOLAS   I'm making Granny a new pillow. It's a present. I'm making it a special old-fashioned way.

NATASHA   *holding up butter coated with feathers*   This is the special old-fashioned way?

NICHOLAS   It's the way she told Ivan about, for his new Project.

NATASHA   Another Project! Tsssk! Now I will blow that school up from its foundations to its weather vane. Since we have no plagues, we must suffer Projects.

NICHOLAS   And, the old fashioned way, before you put the feathers in the pillow, you bake them in the oven to kill all the insects.

NATASHA   *dangerously*   Insects there are in this kitchen who will not fit in that small oven. Who stole the feathers, little feather-cooker?

NICHOLAS   Nobody stole them. Some were from my collection. A few fell out of Granny's hat. Sophie had one or two. Tanya remembered where she'd seen a dead blackbird —

NATASHA   Dead blackbird! **Carrion**! In my **stove**?

HENRY   It does rather put one off the notion of supper.

Sophie and Tanya appear in the doorway. Each carries a serving dish laden with splendid-looking food.

SOPHIE   Supper? Was someone asking after supper? No problem. Here it is, ready.

HENRY   Good Lord. What a splendid spread!

NATASHA   *softly and suspiciously*   Tssssk. Something goes on . . .

HENRY   Nonsense! Don't be so suspicious, Natasha. It's very sweet of them to go to all this effort and lay on a really special supper.

SOPHIE   This isn't special. We eat like this whenever you're out.

HENRY   Nonsense.

SOPHIE   We do. Don't we?

TANYA   Yes.

NICHOLAS   Certainly.

Henry pulls out a chair for **Natasha**.

SOPHIE   Actually, Nicholas usually sits there.

HENRY   Oh, yes. Since when?

SOPHIE   Since ages. Haven't you?

NICHOLAS   Eh? Oh, yes. Yes.

HENRY   I see. *Pulling out another chair*   Is this all right?

SOPHIE   That's fine. Let's eat. I'm starved. Dish it up, Nicholas.

HENRY   These smell delicious. I've not had these particular savouries before.

SOPHIE   Oh, these old things. We have them quite a lot.

TANYA   All the time.

NICHOLAS   I'm getting completely fed up with them, myself.

SOPHIE   But I suppose they are new to you two, yes. You eat in so very rarely these days.

HENRY   *discomfited*   Who made them, anyway?

SOPHIE   Tanya and Nicholas made them tonight. But Ivan is the one who usually does them. He serves them with a rather complicated sauce. But we've just had to manage without that tonight, what with his being too ill to carry on . . .

HENRY   Does Ivan cook like this often, then?

SOPHIE   Oh, no. Not like this. He usually takes much more time and trouble. It's just that, sometimes, when he's exhausted from school, and all his hundreds of extra little jobs from looking after Granny, he has to let the cooking slide a bit. We don't mind, do we?

NICHOLAS   Oh, no.

TANYA   Not at all.

SOPHIE   In fact, we often tell him he ought to slacken off a bit more. We've seen this total physical collapse of his coming for weeks now, haven't we?

TANYA   We **warned** him he was doing too much.

NICHOLAS   Poor old Ivan. He never stops.

SOPHIE   We tell him not to bother. We tell him we'd far rather that he went upstairs for a rest, or tried to get some of his homework done. We say we'd be happy to eat from the chippy. But he insists.

HENRY   Insists? Insists on cooking whenever Natasha and I are both out? **Ivan**?

SOPHIE   He won't let us help, either. We offer all the time, but he keeps saying our homework and swimming and music are far, far too important to miss. He won't let us share hardly any of the work, will he?

TANY   No.

NICHOLAS   Hardly any.

SOPHIE   He says that it's important to him.

TANYA   Yes, that's what he says.

NICHOLAS   Yes, that's what Ivan always says.

SOPHIE   That it's the very least that he can do for us, considering . . .

HENRY   Considering what?

NATASHA   *still soft and suspicious*   Tssss.

SOPHIE   Oh, look. You've finished. Bring the puff pastry pies over, Tanya.

HENRY   They look **fantastic**.

SOPHIE   A little disappointing. But never mind.

TANYA   Not quite as good as Ivan's, no.

NICHOLAS   Ivan's pastry is spectacular.

TANYA   Of course, he's had far more practice making it than any of us have.

NICHOLAS   He's got the knack of rolling it out right.

SOPHIE   A very steady, experienced touch.

HENRY   So who made it tonight?

SOPHIE   We all did. I made the spinach and beef filling, and Nicholas made the pastry, and Tanya put it all together.

TANYA   Nowhere near as neatly as Ivan does, though.

SOPHIE   Well, Tanya, Ivan spends much more time than you do on this sort of thing. You have your homework, after all . . .

NATASHA   Tssssk.

HENRY   Ivan has homework too, surely!

SOPHIE   Oh, Ivan! He's totally given up on homework these days. He has a shocking backlog — weeks and weeks. He says he's too discouraged to try any longer. After all, he's always worked hard and done very well in school, before he got too tired and strained and frazzled to be able to concentrate on any of it any more. He used to be so capable. And now! To start failing after all these years of steady A grades . . .

HENRY   Failing? My Ivan? **Ivan**? I can hardly **believe** it! Nobody has mentioned anything to me about this. Are you sure?

SOPHIE   He doesn't **mind**, does he?

TANYA   Oh, no.

NICHOLAS   He doesn't mind at all.

HENRY   I mind. I mind a **lot**.

SOPHIE   Well, Ivan doesn't. He puts us first, you see. He says that there's always a slim chance that he may some day get another chance to educate himself. But **we** only have one chance to grow up in a secure and nurturing family environment. He wouldn't want the rest of us to miss that. Ivan says that a regular and comforting home background, with supporting rituals and systems, is doubly vital for the psychologically orphaned.

HENRY   Psychologically **orphaned**?

SOPHIE   That's right. He's thought about these things a good deal, Ivan has, and we've done work on it in Social Science. There are a lot of articles about the effects on children of family deprivation and loss.

HENRY   Deprivation and loss?

SOPHIE   And separation and abandonment.

HENRY   Separation? **Abandonment**?

SOPHIE   You're never **here**, you know. You're always **out**.

TANYA   Always out.

NICHOLAS   **Always**.

HENRY   Oh, God! I feel simply **awful**!

SOPHIE   *sweetly*   Perhaps you've been overdoing it, like

Ivan. Perhaps you'll come down with the same shocking virus that's mowed him down . . .

Natasha covers her face with her hands, and bursts into tears.
Henry comforts her. The children grin at one another,
unnoticed. Ivan walks in, blowing his nose.

HENRY   Ivan! Sit down. Take my place. Try to eat. One mouthful. Just to please me, **please.**

IVAN   Gosh, these look good. Are these the ones you can buy — **ouch!**

Ivan rubs his shin under the table, glaring at Sophie.

HENRY   Never mind that now. We have decisions to make. Natasha, my love. Stop weeping. Everything's going to be put right.

IVAN   What's going on here?

SOPHIE   Be quiet and listen. You might hear something to your advantage.

HENRY   Things must change. Now. From today, either your mother or I will be in the house most weekday evenings. I'll give up woodwork. I've learned enough to make bookshelves, and bookshelves is all we really needed. Natasha, when you sign on for Advanced Italian, make sure to choose the Saturday session. Meanwhile, we'll cut down on the dancing.

NATASHA   Oh, Henry! I did so adore all the dancing!

HENRY   We'll still go every Saturday night. And Thursdays, perhaps. But we'll give up all the classes where I was working on my turns.

TANYA   You could stick to disco dancing, where turns don't matter.

NICHOLAS   Unless you're turning green.

SOPHIE   We should get an order book from the grocery. Lots of people have them. Whenever you notice something's nearly gone, you write it down. And, bingo, once a week a box of goodies gets dumped on your doorstep.

NATASHA   I'll sell that antique dresser in the hall. I never liked it. I'll buy a huge, white, gleaming freezer with the money.

TANYA   And fill it with heavenly convenience foods!

SOPHIE   Come on. Let's clear the dresser out before anybody starts changing their mind. Come on, all of you. Everyone.

*They all troop out, except for **Nicholas**, who turns to the audience:*

NICHOLAS   So there we were. All change all over again. And this time it really looked as if it might work out well, with nobody doing more than a fair share, and nobody feeling cheated or tricked or blackmailed. Quite the best way. We could have gone on like that for ever. But no. The doctor had to come and spoil everything . . .

The children appear at corners of the room, eavesdropping.

IVAN   *to **Nicholas***   Is the Doctor still in there?

NICHOLAS   He's been with Granny all this time.

TANYA   They're coming out!

*The children duck down behind the chairs. **Natasha** and **Henry** accompany the **Doctor** from Granny's room across to the door.*

DOCTOR   Of course, the syndrome is remarkably common. Common enough to have been nicknamed 'The Old Man's Friend'. It involves severe inflammation of the mucous membrane, affects the bronchial tubes, maxillary sinuses, respiratory passages, and there you have it in no time at all — broncho-pneumonia. I don't have to tell you, in someone of Mrs Harris's age, the prognosis can't be an optimistic one. No, I'm afraid it can't be. It can't be . . .

They go out, shaking their heads.

TANYA   There! Broncho-pneumonia! She's caught Ivan's cold, and now she's going to die of it.

SOPHIE   That isn't nice.

TANYA   It's true, though, isn't it?

IVAN   She may not die.

TANYA   You heard what he just said. He said pneumonia was called 'The Old Man's Friend'.

IVAN   He's only a doctor. He doesn't know everything.

TANYA   He sounded confident enough about this. It will seem strange when Granny's gone. Having an extra room downstairs, and not having to keep quiet and carry trays through all the time.

IVAN She's not dead yet!

NICHOLAS Do you remember when she still ate with us? And if you put your elbows on the table, she'd shake her knife at you and tell you all meat joints on the table would be carved, cooked or not.

SOPHIE She said punks looked like half-scraped carrots.

TANYA She used to say: 'Little girl, box of paints, sucked her brush, joined the Saints!'

SOPHIE Do you remember the day she actually sat in Nicholas's paddling pool in the garden, wearing that funny orange bathing dress with the little frilly skirts?

NICHOLAS And you and Ivan came through the gate with your new pet rabbit! She sat in the water saying: 'The pig that has two owners will die of hunger.'

TANYA It did, too.

IVAN
SOPHIE } Oh, shut up, Tanya!

SOPHIE Do you remember when she bopped the new milkman on the head with a bottle for cheating?

TANYA And when she called the Detective Inspector 'a young whipper-snapper'?

NICHOLAS And when Tanya showed her brand new shoes, and Granny called them 'pretty little shoe-poddies'?

SOPHIE And Tanya never wore them again!

TANYA She said Mrs Herbert was so bandy-legged, she couldn't have stopped a pig in a doorway.

SOPHIE She said, when Nicholas was born, he looked no bigger than half a pound of soap after a good day's wash!

NICHOLAS She was so **funny**.

IVAN She isn't dead yet!

*Henry and **Natasha** return from seeing out the **Doctor**.*

IVAN Is she? She isn't dead yet. They're making out she's dead already and Tanya even thinks I killed her. But she's not dead yet!

NATASHA The Doctor thinks she may well die.

IVAN What does he know about it? He's only guessing.

HENRY She is ill, Ivan. And she's eighty-seven.

NICHOLAS 'Thou shalt come to thy grave in a full age, like as a shock of corn cometh in his season.'

Everyone stares at **Nicholas***.*

HENRY Where on earth did you pick that up?

NICHOLAS At school. We did a Project on Death when the hamster pegged out.

HENRY *shaking his head* Astonishing!

NATASHA Tssssk . . .

TANYA Is Granny really dying? Can we see her?

NICHOLAS I'd like to give her the pillow I made for her. I know if she's dying she won't be needing it much longer; but still I'd like to give it to her.

HENRY Come on then. But you must remember she's very weak. Only two at a time. Youngest first.

Tanya and **Nicholas** *follow* **Natasha** *and* **Henry** *into Granny's bedroom.* **Sophie** *and* **Ivan** *are left alone.* **Sophie** *picks up* **Ivan***'s Granny Project, and starts leafing through it.*

SOPHIE Ivan.

IVAN What?

SOPHIE You learned a lot from Granny, didn't you?

IVAN Mmmm. Yes, I did.

SOPHIE What was the most important thing you learned? *Holding out the Project* Is it in here?

IVAN No, not in there. Everything in there is interesting — at least to me. But what she said that was important is not the sort of stuff you put in a Project.

SOPHIE What sort of stuff was it?

IVAN Well . . . She talked quite a bit about being old.

SOPHIE What did she say?

IVAN She said that for the first time in her life, she had time to herself. Time to sit quietly and watch the plants grow, she said. Time to keep still so all the birds came near. She said some days she sat in her chair and watched Natasha rushing about pegging sheets on the washing line,and then she would sit quietly the livelong day, and watch them dry.

SOPHIE Watched them dry? All day?

IVAN And listened.

SOPHIE Listened?

IVAN That's what she said. She listened to them flapping in the wind. *He waves his hands in the air* Flap-flap, flap-flap. That's what she said. She said if you get to sit quietly in a house for long enough, you get to feel a part of it.

SOPHIE I'll never be like that.

IVAN That's what she said. She thought she'd never be like that. She said all those years when she and grandfather would stay up till all hours doing the union work, fighting the battles over pay, and conditions, and health insurance, she never thought of simply living her life with him quietly, alone, just being together like two companionable cows in a field.

SOPHIE If there's work to be done, you have to do it, simply because it's there, still waiting to be done.

IVAN Oh, yes. But she says they weren't hard-boiled revolutionaries. They were soft souls.

SOPHIE Soft souls?

IVAN She meant that they were proud of little things. Like the fact children don't cough all through the winters any more, or walk around crying from chilblains. She said making things better is sad, slow work, and you have to be very careful not to mix it all up with fancy ideas.

SOPHIE Fancy ideas?

IVAN Like being a revolutionary, or something.

SOPHIE You always have to keep the chilblains in mind?

IVAN I think that's what she meant. Always to remember what's going to mean the most to most people.

SOPHIE I've never even seen a chilblain.

IVAN *Grinning* A revolution fought and won!

SOPHIE Ivan.

IVAN What?

SOPHIE If we could go back to the beginning and start again, would you still vote for keeping Granny at home?

IVAN Yes.

SOPHIE Just the same?

IVAN No, not just the same. Not with the system where they did all the work, or with the one where I did. I'd choose what we decided in the end.

SOPHIE The worked-out plan?

IVAN Right. That was good. That would have worked. And we were stupid not to have worked that out before.

SOPHIE Really stupid.

IVAN One consolation, though. We're never going to be that stupid again. Because I've decided I'm going to be a union man, like Grandfather. I'm going into Negotiation.

SOPHIE Start practising on the family?

IVAN Work my way up.

SOPHIE Today, 49 Bonnington Road; tomorrow the National Conciliation Board!

IVAN Don't scoff.

SOPHIE I'm not. I think that you'd be very good at it.

IVAN I think I would.

SOPHIE Ivan, do you believe there's any purpose in life?

IVAN Not really, no.

SOPHIE But you've decided what you're going to do.

IVAN It's not a purpose. I just thought I might try to improve things a little.

SOPHIE That is a purpose.

IVAN I suppose it is.

SOPHIE You've got one, then.

IVAN I suppose I have.

SOPHIE A sort of Project for Life.

IVAN Don't let Mum hear, for God's sake.

*While they are laughing, Granny's door is opened by **Natasha**, who beckons the two of them inside. They give each other one last grin before, with solemn faces, they walk into Granny's room.*

STAGING THE PLAY

A successful production of *The Granny Project* will depend on the audience being totally convinced by the six members of the Harris family. If the characters, and the relationships between them, are believable and natural, then the audience will be convinced that Granny is just off-stage.

Concentrate on developing well-established characters so that the audience will feel like a fly on the wall watching a real family in its kitchen. You should aim for an effect which critics might describe as *verisimilitude* or as near to the *truth* as possible.

In rehearsal, move away from the script and improvise some of the scenes so that if you forget your lines you will have the confidence to continue speaking in character. Also, build your character by constructing his or her past life. Make a list of *facts* such as your age, achievements, likes, dislikes and personal qualities. As a family, decide how long Granny has lived with you, what aspects of your life together, such as holidays, have been restricted by her presence, and what positive contributions she has made to the family.

If you are playing one of the adults, do not simply resort to drawing stiff facial lines using make-up to suggest your age. Instead, try to find one element in the character to emphasise their adulthood. The young doctor relies on medical jargon to hide his lack of confidence; Henry appears long suffering and tired in contrast to Natasha who seems to have dynamism and energy. Your characterisation will be helped by naturalistic costume and props which should be easy to assemble. Your stage set can be absolutely naturalistic, or it can be suggested by only a few props, i.e. notional. The play can be performed successfully on your school stage or *in the round* on the Hall floor.

If you decide to use the proscenium arch style of production, as many school performances do, then a boxed set would be impressive, especially if it looks like a real kitchen with one *transparent* wall. You could design it as shown in the diagram.

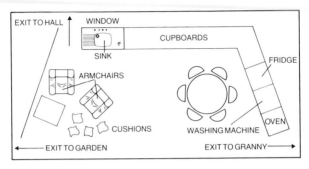

Naturalistic set for a proscenium style stage

The lighting plot could create a simple, interior atmosphere throughout the play. It could also appear more complicated and effective if you light the window on the upstage flat from behind to suggest different times of the day.

If you prefer a notional set in the round, all you need really is a table, stools and perhaps a few cushions on the floor to create a variety of levels. If the height of the table restricts the audience's view, you might solve it by putting the audience on three sides and the table against a wall.

Your acting can convey the smell of the soiled sheets behind the door off-stage, while Natasha can discover the roasting feathers off-stage and re-enter with an offending handful. As long as your character is convincing, your audience will not be concerned with any imperfections in your set. They will be too busy enjoying the play to notice.

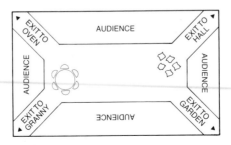

Suggestion for a notional set in the round

ACTIVITIES ON AND AROUND THE PLAY

DRAMA BASED ON THE SCRIPT

1 Medical opinions

Organisation: Work in pairs or groups of three. Re-read the
doctor's remarks about Granny's ailments on *pages 2 and
3*.

Situation: The doctor is giving Granny his opinion about her
condition, using many long words and scientific
explanations. Another member of the family joins in, with
details of Granny's eccentric behaviour. Granny has a
logical explanation for everything, as well as her own
opinions of the kind of treatment she should be getting.

Opening line: FAMILY MEMBER: Why do you always insist on
wearing one slipper and one shoe when you come into the
kitchen, Granny?

2 Where is your homework?

Organisation: Work in pairs. One of you will be Jo Finch,
Ivan's Social Studies teacher. The other is Ivan.

Situation: Ivan has successfully blackmailed Henry and his
project has been burnt. How will he explain a missing
term's homework? How does Ivan, one of the brightest
students, feel when he is made to appear lazy by a
disappointed teacher?

Opening line: JO FINCH: And where is your project, Ivan?

3 Old friends

Organisation: Work with a partner. One of you will be Granny,
and the other will be an old friend, who has come to visit
her.

Situation: Granny confides in her friend about the behaviour of the Harris family. How does she feel about the way they treat her? How does she respond when the children take over the work of looking after her? What advice can her friend give her?

Opening line: GRANNY: No, I'm not imagining things. The family are behaving very strangely.

4   Henry and Natasha 'on the town'

Organisation: One of you is Henry and the other is Natasha.

Situation: The new organisation of the household has been going on for some time. How do you both feel about the changes in family life? Do you feel guilt or relief? What worries do you still have about the situation?

Opening line: HENRY: I think responsibility is good for children.

5   What will the neighbours think?

Organisation: Work in a group of three or four. Decide who will be Henry and who will be Natasha. The other members of the group are neighbours of the family who are curious about the new life which they seem to be leading.

Situation: The neighbours meet the Harris's late one night, coming out of the dance hall.

Opening line: NEIGHBOUR: And how's your mother, Mr Harris?

6   Responsibilities

Organisation: In groups of three or four decide who will be each of the children in the Harris family. Characters: Ivan, Tanya, Nicholas and Sophie. The children have split the household tasks between them but several of the tasks have been left undone — Granny's window has been left open, and her hot water bottles have not been filled. She seems to have caught a chill. Whose fault is it?

Opening line: TANYA: It's not my fault, Ivan. I had to write my essay.

7   Caring for Granny

Organisation: Work in pairs. One of you will be Granny and the other one will be one of the Harris children.

Situation: It's your turn to clear up Granny's room. Granny is a bit confused. Although she has just eaten, she insists she hasn't and demands lunch. How can you convince her that she's had her lunch, without becoming impatient or angry?

Opening line: GRANNY: Stop fiddling around over there. I'm hungry. When will lunch be ready?

8 Ivan the Terrorist

Organisation: Work in a small group. Re-read the end of Act One and the beginning of Act Two, when Ivan is accused of blackmail by the other children and Henry.

Situation: After his confrontation with Ivan, Henry has had a nightmare in which he imagines that Ivan has grown up and become a terrorist, perhaps 'dying from bullets or starving himself to death in some cell', as he says in the play.

Using movement and sound as well as speech, show Henry's dream of Ivan as a terrorist. Remember that dreams are rarely naturalistic, so that the sounds and movements you use can be repeated and exaggerated to create a nightmare effect.

9 Making changes

Organisation: Work in a small group of three or four. You are a team of television newsreaders and reporters. Introduce other characters as you need them.

Situation: Imagine that Ivan, as he says in the last scene of the play, has given his life to union work and making things better for other people.

Prepare and show a series of news headlines, perhaps accompanied by brief interviews, which will show us the progress of Ivan's adult life. What kind of events does he get involved with in his efforts to bring about change? How successful is he at the work he has chosen?

10 Growing old

Organisation: Work with a partner.

Situation: Discuss the four children in the Harris family. Which of them do you find the most interesting? Do you identify with any one of them? What do you think each of them will become when they grow up? Don't forget to consider the clues we are given about their different characters in the play.

Now, imagine that one of you (A) is one of the Harris children, but at a time in their life when they are growing old. Your partner (B) is a young relative or friend who wants to know about your early life. What will you tell them? How will you remember the Granny Project?

DISCUSSION

1a What does Sophie mean when she says at the end of Act One that the 'end can never justify the means'? Do you think she is right?

b Can you find any examples from recent events in the news where people seem to feel that the opposite is true?

2a Does anything in the play remind you of your own family life?

b How are chores divided in your family?

c Do you think that your arrangement is a good one?

d How might it be improved?

3a The Harris children took action to try to change something they didn't agree with. Is there anything you see around you which you think is wrong?

b Can you think of any way in which you could take action to change things you don't agree with?

FURTHER WORK

1 Choose familiar television actors and cast them as characters in the play. What does your choice indicate about your view of each character in the play?

2 Design a stage set for *The Granny Project*. You could always use magazine photographs if you find drawing difficult.

3 Design Granny's room as a separate stage set, showing the difference between her furniture and the Harris's. Think of five or six 'props' which might be important in helping to create

Granny's character. Either draw them or choose pictures from magazines to represent them. Try to find one actual object which might have meaning for an old person, for example a photograph or a wedding ring. Tell the group why you have chosen it and what it means.

4 Pick out the climax or the main high points in the script. Where are they and how have they been created? Through humour? Or tension?

5 Why do you think the author has chosen not to present Granny on stage? What difference would it make to the play if she did appear? Does her absence make us more sympathetic towards her?

6 Work with one or two friends. Look at the section 'Story of a Lifetime' on *page* 70. Can you devise a similar page to cover the events in Granny's life? Some of the facts are in the play, but you may have to invent some details which you feel will fit in with what we are told about Granny.

7 Compare your version of Granny's life with those done by other groups. What similarities and differences are there?

8 Work with a partner. Discuss how you think Henry and Natasha managed to meet and get married. Choose to be either Henry or Natasha, and write a letter to a friend describing the first meeting and what your reaction is to it.

FROM NOVEL TO PLAYSCRIPT

When Anne Fine dramatised her novel *The Granny Project*, she omitted the following extract. Before Ivan completes his project, Natasha and Henry hold a dinner party to impress Henry's headmaster. Tanya has a 'nightmare' as part of their campaign and Granny, woken by the noise, enters the dining room:

Peach-and-feather sorbet

Natasha came from a family who knew what real bad times were: failed harvests, men in uniform, barbed wire at snow covered border posts, night knocks upon the door. She found herself recovering much faster than Henry.

'Adelaide!' she cried. 'Here just in time for heavenly dessert. Find one more chair, Henry. Do help your mother. Take off her hat.'

As Mrs Harris struggled with her hatpins, a shower of blue feathers shimmered through the air and landed on the pretty china dishes heaped high with fresh peach sorbet. Picking one more than usually motheaten specimen off his own serving, Henry's headmaster said:

'Have you come very far, Mrs Harris?'

'No distance at all,' Henry's mother assured him. 'The shortest of walks. I can do it in no time.'

'That's wonderful.'

'Quite wonderful.'

'I'm most impressed.'

The chorus was spontaneous. The talk, all at once, was of what a marvel Henry's mother must be, to make her way on foot at eighty-seven through that perplexing labyrinth out there of Bonnington Circles and Crescents and Closes and Drives, in the pitch dark, and still arrive in time for dessert.

Mrs Harris swelled with the appreciation. She spooned up fresh peach sorbet and feathers and tried hard to concentrate as Henry's headmaster warmly and encouragingly compared her capabilities most favourably with those of his own elderly relations. She lost the thread for a moment when her teeth slipped; but when she realised that Henry's headmaster, instead of continuing to detail her own virtues had, like a vast dam suddenly unblocked, simply taken to abusing his own ageing mother, she let the cold of sorbet on her new teeth block up her ears entirely. Ivan, outside the door, heard it all; but even at his breakneck scribble he could not get it all down, word for word. He was reduced, by the sheer speed and richness of the anecdotes, to taking only the briefest of notes to flesh out later, more at his leisure.

'. . . hides the apostle spoons in the flour bin . . .'

Ivan scribbled fast.

'. . . tips all the pills out and puts them into other bottles, treats them like Smarties . . . . phoned up a dozen times that evening . . . . took the thing out of the dustbin again and wore it to the Prizegiving, covered in peelings . . . . and when I got there, through all that snow and black ice, all that was wrong was that the volume was turned down . . . . and gets through quarts of sherry, don't know how she does it, never seems drunk . . . . . they won't deliver to her house any more, simply can't stand the constant scenes . . . . and I've been married to Martha for over twenty-two years now, but will my mother remember Martha's name? No,. she will not . . . . the same book in her lap for four years now. What? What's the title? I don't know. The Life of Mary, Queen of Scots, I believe. I haven't read it. I don't think she has either, to tell you the truth. It's upside down as often as not . . . . found seven wills, and each had a different member of the family cut off without a penny . . . . used to let her eat with us until she took to taking out her dentures and plonking them down on the table, next to her plate . . . . hates the Health Visitor, I do believe she'd climb out of her coffin to punch her . . . . lists of things in bundles and hides them all over the bungalow. They've got to calling her The Squirrel on the estate . . . . . turned out it wasn't broken at all, she'd just switched it off at the wall plug, by mistake . . . . .'

Spilled, relieved, drained, the flood waters dropped steadily:

'. . . . been close to killing her at times. I know I shouldn't say it but it's true . . . . . a hair's breadth from matricide on several occasions . . . . . looked at the kitchen knife, truly I have, and . . . . . shouldn't go on about it really, sure I'm boring you . . . . . just can't imagine the sheer strain of it all . . . .'

49

Henry gazed across the table and into his headmaster's eyes, appalled by the stories he had heard, suffused with admiration for this man who suffered as he suffered, but worse. Natasha leaned on her bare white elbows, contented, watching her guests behind their empty sorbet dishes and little piles of blue feathers, watching in still fascination as Henry's headmaster's deep feeling tirade slowly abated. They'd most of them known Henry's headmaster for years, and never heard him talking like this. No one had ever smashed through that chilly reserve before. But trust it all to happen at Natasha's! Trust that exotic Russian passion to spread around a dinner table as though it were catching! What tales! What guests! What food! Down to the feathers in the sorbet!

Henry's mother's hearing came back as her new teeth warmed. She looked up hopefully. She'd not refuse another helping of that delicious peach and feather sorbet, but that demented man across the table was still going on and on about his poor mother. If no one else here was capable of stemming the tide, then it was clearly up to her.

'Oh, she does sound a *trial*,' said Mrs Harris. 'But I think I may safely say I've been no trouble to *my* son.'

Henry, transfixed still, answered automatically.

'That's right, Mum. Been no trouble. None at all.'

DISCUSSION

1 Why do you think the headmaster felt he could confide in the Harris family? Do you sympathise with him?

2 If you had only read the section that starts ' . . . been close to killing her' would you take a different view of the headmaster? Do you think *The Granny Project* has made you think differently about the problems of old age? Why?

3 Are you made uncomfortable by the way in which the headmaster's problems with his mother come across as humorous to us? Do you think people often laugh at things that are serious or sad? Why? Can you think of any example?

4 Why would this scene be difficult to include in the play? Try to think of as many reasons as possible.

DRAMA

1 Home, Sweet Home

Organisation: Work with a partner. One of you is Henry's
headmaster's mother. The other is an old friend of hers.

Situation: The headmaster's mother tells her friend some of
her complaints about her son. The old friend may be in a
similar situation and is sympathetic. She/he may even
have some advice to give.

Opening line: MOTHER: He never stops complaining!

2 The dinner party expanded

Organisation: In groups of five or seven, decide which of the
following characters you will be:

> *Henry Harris*: teacher who wants to be Head of Modern
> Languages
> *Natasha Harris*: his Russian wife
> *Adelaide Harris*: Henry's mother who lives with them
> *James Evans*: Henry's headmaster
> *Martha Evans*: James Evans's wife
> The following characters are optional:
> *Robert Higgins*: Ten years younger than Henry; also
> wants to be Head of Modern Languages
> *Fiona Higgins*: Robert's wife

For these unfamiliar characters, you must decide on their
ages, jobs, their relationship with Henry and Natasha.

Situation: Set up your scene with chairs around a dinner table
with an extra chair for Granny, who is standing in the
doorway.

Develop the scene following the shape of the extract and
expanding the roles of your new characters. The
Headmaster can make up his own stories about his
mother's eccentric behaviour and he need not rely on the
extract.

Opening line: NATASHA: Adelaide, you're just in time for
dessert. Henry, get your mother a chair.

Using some of the lines and ideas developed in your
improvisation, script the scene, including stage directions and
a description of the set.

WHAT DOES OLD AGE MEAN TO YOU?

False Statements About Grannies

Often wicked tales are told
Of grannies being very old
Hard of hearing, poor of sight
With teeth that can no longer bite
Stiff old joints and snow white hair
But don't believe them
They're not fair.

Grannies can watch TV while they sleep.

Some grannies have whiskers.

Some grannies have wrinkly faces.

Yes, dear, if you are a good girl and eat up all your cabbage.

Why are you so wrinkly granny?

Will I have whiskers too?

What's so special about whiskers?

Some grannies dye their hair.

Some grannies smell of moth balls.

Some grannies wear corsets.

Some very special grannies can even take their teeth out!

clack! clack!

Wow!

Brill!

Brave face on it

From Mrs John Miller

Sir, Your travel article (February 2) referred three times to elderly skiers as 'wrinklies'. As one whose face is fairly liberally creased I do not shrink from reality, but I find the growing use of this word to describe old people both patronising and rude.

We do not, after all, refer to our teenage friends as 'acknies': a little reciprocal politeness would be nice.

Yours faithfully
CHRISTIAN MILLER

Brave face on it

From Mr Charles Wolfe Keene

Sir, Your correspondent, Mrs John Miller (February 7), should not despair. 'Oldies' today start at 25: 'wrinklies' follow at 35. After 45 she may have cause to worry: she then becomes a 'crumblie'!

Yours faithfully
CHARLES WOLFE KEENE

Brave face on it

From Dr Margaret McLachlan

Sir, While I agree with Mrs Miller (February 7) that the term 'wrinklies' (of which I am one) is discourteous and unpleasing, I must in all honesty confess that in my profession, although we don't refer to our teenagers as 'acknies', we do refer to them as 'pimplies'.

Yours faithfully
MARGARET McLACHLAN

1   Look at the extracts above and list all the words and phrases you can think of associated with old age e.g. OAP, wrinkled.

2   Write down as many sayings or proverbs as you can think of which concern old age. What views do they present of old age?

3   Which of the proverbs below do you think give an accurate picture of ageing?

- Young men think old men are fools; but old men know young men are fools.

- Young people don't know what age is, and old people forget what youth was.

- Young men may die but old men must die.

- No man loves life like him that's growing old.

- Age does not give sense, it only makes one go slower.

- Age steals all things, even the mind.

4 Look at the photographs and decide:

a Which of these personal qualities you would put with each photograph. You can relate them to both, if you like:

HONEST   AGGRESSIVE   GENEROUS   WISE   GOOD-LOOKING
EVEN-TEMPERED   DEMANDING   ENTERTAINING   CHARMING
AWKWARD   INTELLIGENT   KIND   HAPPY   COMPLAINING
HELPFUL   ATHLETIC   SCATTY   WEALTHY   IN-LOVE
AMBITIOUS

b Whether either or both would be suitable for the following occupations:

PARK KEEPER   BANK MANAGER   THIEF   POSTMAN   BUS
DRIVER   FACTORY WORKER   SOLICITOR   SPORTS' REPORTER
SPY   MEMBER OF PARLIAMENT   CLEANER   SHOP ASSISTANT
STAR IN A LOVE FILM   SCIENTIST   PIANIST   ACTOR
COMPUTER EXPERT   VET   DOCTOR

DISCUSSION

- Which personal qualities are specific to old people?
- Which personal qualities are common to both young *and* old people?
- When do young people become old, and what happens to their personalities?
- Which jobs do we tend to associate with old people?
- Which jobs cannot be done by old people?
- Do all people retire at 60 or 65?
- What do you think you will be like when *you* retire?

WRITING

1   Think of an old person you know and complete the following list:

If my grandma/grandpa/friend were a colour she/he would be ....

If my grandma/grandpa/friend were a flower she/he would be ....

If my grandma/grandpa/friend were a car she/he would be ....

If my grandma/grandpa/friend were a vegetable she/he would be ....

If my grandma/grandpa/friend were a piece of furniture she/he would be ....

If my grandma/grandpa/friend were an animal she/he would be ....

If my grandma/grandpa/friend were a TV personality she/he would be ....

2   Imagine this same old person sitting in a chair or standing at a window and try to describe them in one paragraph, perhaps using the images you have created. Think also of how they would be dressed, the objects which might be near them, and the kind of room they might be in. All of these things will help to create a picture of the kind of person they are.

3   Now do the same character study of someone your own age and compare the different images you have used.

4   What do the two descriptions reveal about your own attitudes to old age?

5   Using your first character study as a basis, write *either* a short story called 'The Face at the Window' *or* called 'Retirement Day — The Best Day of My Life'.

6   Using your second character study as a basis, write a short story called 'It's Tough to be a Teenager' or 'Happy Days'.

Over the Top at Sixty?

* Barbara Cartland writes 25 novels a year at 81
* Laurence Olivier played King Lear at 75
* Ronald Reagan was re-elected President of the USA at 74
* Winston Churchill retired from being Prime Minister at 80
* Mrs Winifred Clark married 80 year-old Albert Smith the day before her 100th birthday
* In 1985 the oldest man in the world was 119 year-old Mr Izumi of Japan who began work in 1872 and retired 98 years later!
* The Queen Mother flew on Concorde as an 85th birthday treat.

You don't have to be old to get a Senior Citizen's Railcard. You just have to be 60.

Pat Phoenix, and anyone else who's reached 60, can get train tickets at up to 50% off. Details from stations, post offices and travel agents.

We're getting there ⧚

The railcard advertisement exploits the fact that the actress Pat Phoenix is a long way from being the stereotyped OAP we might expect to apply for a card.

Design your own advertisement for a car or a cosmetic product aimed at older customers which does not present them as stereotypes.

OLD AGE IN LITERATURE

Read the following extract from *Cider with Rosie* by Laurie Lee.

For several more years the lives of the two old ladies continued to revolve in intimate enmity around each other. Like cold twin stars, linked but divided, they survived by a mutual balance. Both of them reached back similarly in time, shared the same modes and habits, the same sense of feudal order, the same rampaging terrible God. *They were far more alike than unalike, and could not abide each other.*

They arranged things therefore so that they never met. They used separate paths when they climbed the bank, they shopped on different days, they relieved themselves in different areas, and staggered their church-going hours. But each one knew always what the other was up to, and passionately disapproved. Granny Wallon worked at her flowering vats, boiling and blending her wines; or crawled through her cabbages; or tapped on our windows, gossiped, complained, or sang. Granny Trill continued to rise in the dark, comb her waxen hair, sit out in the wood, chew, sniff and suck up porridge, and study her almanac. Yet between them they sustained a mutual awareness based solely on ear and nostril. When Granny Wallon's wines boiled, Granny Trill had convulsions; when Granny Trill took snuff, Granny Wallon had strictures — and neither let the other forget it. So all day they listened, sniffed and pried, rapping on floors and ceilings, and prowled their rooms with hawking coughs, chivvying each other long-range. It was a tranquil, bitter–pleasant life, perfected by years of custom; and to me they both seemed everlasting, deathless crones of an eternal mythology; they had always been somewhere there in the wainscot and I could imagine no world without them.

Then one day, as Granny Trill was clambering out of her wood, she stumbled and broke her hip. She went to bed then for ever. She lay patient and yellow in a calico coat, her combed hair fine as a girl's. She accepted her doom without complaint, as though some giant authority — Squire, father, or God — had ordered her there to receive it.

'I knowed it was coming,' she told our Mother, 'after that visitation. I saw it last week sitting at the foot of me bed. Some person in white; I dunno . . . '

There was a sharp early rap on our window next morning. Granny Wallon was bobbing outside.

'Did you hear him, missus?' she asked knowingly. 'He been a-screeching around since midnight.' The death-bird was Granny Wallon's private pet and messenger, and she gave a skip as she told us about him. 'He called three-a-four times. Up in them yews. Her's going, you mark my words.'

And that day indeed Granny Trill died, whose bones were too old to mend. *Like a delicate pale bubble, blown a little higher and further than the other girls of her generation,* she had floated just long enough for us to catch sight of her, had hovered for an instant before our eyes; and then had popped suddenly, and disappeared for ever, leaving nothing on the air but a faint-drying image and the tiniest cloud of snuff.

The little church was packed for her funeral, for the old lady had been a landmark. They carried her coffin along the edge of the wood and then drew it on a cart through the village. Granny Wallon, dressed in a shower of jets, followed some distance behind; and during the service she kept to the back of the church and everybody admired her.

All went well till the lowering of the coffin, when there was a sudden and distressing commotion. Granny Wallon, ribbons flying, her bonnet awry, fought her way to the side of the grave.

'It's a lie!' she screeched, pointing down at the coffin. 'That baggage were younger'n me! 95, she says! — ain't more'n 90, an' I gone on 92! It's a crime you letting 'er go to 'er Maker got up in such brazen lies! Dig up the old devil! Get 'er brass plate off! It's insulting the living church! . . . '

They carried her away, struggling and crying, kicking out with her steel-sprung boots. Her cries grew fainter and were soon obliterated by the sounds of the grave-diggers' spades. The clump of clay falling on Granny Trill's coffin sealed her with her inscription for ever; for no one knew the truth of her age, there was no one old enough to know. •

Granny Wallon had triumphed, she had buried her rival; and now there was no more to do. From then on she faded and diminished daily, kept to her house and would not be seen. Sometimes we heard mysterious knocks in the night, rousing and summoning sounds. But the days were silent, no one walked in the garden, or came skipping to claw at our window. The wine fires sank and died in the kitchen, as did the sweet fires of obsession.

About two weeks later, of no special disease, Granny Wallon gave up in her sleep. She was found on her bed, dressed in bonnet and shawl, with her signalling broom in her hand. Her open eyes were fixed on the ceiling in a listening stare of death. *There was nothing in fact to keep her alive; no cause, no bite, no fury.* Er-Down-Under had joined Er-Up-Atop, having lived closer than anyone knew.

DISCUSSION

1 *'They were far more alike than unalike, and could not abide each other.'* What do you think of this statement? Have you ever thought this a possible reason for two people not getting along? It might help to think about your own family.

2 *'Like a delicate pale bubble, blown a little higher and further than the others girls of her generation . . .'* Does this description of Granny Trill come as a surprise after what we have learned about her? Why? What effect does this description have on you at this point?

3 Tanya in *The Granny Project* says about Granny going into a Home; *'And in the end, she'll just give up and die.'* The author in this extract says of Granny Wallon; *'There was nothing in fact to keep her alive; no cause, no bite, no fury.'* Do you believe that old people can simply lose the will to live?

DRAMA

Mediating

Preparation: Read the 'Cider with Rosie' extract carefully.

Organisation: Work in groups of three. One of you is a neighbour who would like to help the two Grannies to resolve their differences. The other two are the Grannies.

Situation: The neighbour tries to persuade Granny Trill or Granny Wallon to be more tolerant. Alternatively, you might try to persuade one of the two to move to another cottage.

Opening line: NEIGHBOUR: Why don't you try to get along with each other?

59

The next poem describes a visit by the poet to his elderly parents. He takes his wife, Ada, and young son with him.

Bill

It was right for us,
that square, its flaking dignity
sealed from the rest of Islington, with Em
just round the corner, and home
near enough to drop in,
too far away
for stopping.

And when we did call, and saw the old girl
slommocking in curlers, and dad
remote with illness, stuck forever
in his armchair by the fire,
his fine face
drawn with his fight for breath, silent
with the disgrace

of what he'd let things come to, and kids
and slovenly neighbours
hanging about as if the place was theirs —
I sat miserable, with Ada tense
fussing over the kid,
brushing them off him, irritable,
wanting to be rid

of their snotty noses, their yowled
words, their itching heads, as if
he'd catch not only fleas from them, but
the manners of them, the voices, clothes, the
stunted, sad
adulthood of tough, neglected kids.
I was glad

to be there once; we'd found
my father only, propped by the fire,
a heap of sticks just within reach, some stout
in a cup in the grate. His old
and natural charm
flowered in the peace we brought him.
He raised an arm

and Ada gave the kid. We sat and watched
the old man with our cradled baby
as the tarred wood flared and bubbled.
And then he talked — dry voiced, the breath
halting his words —
to the baby, not to us. He told
of great seabirds

that followed clippers in the China seas
and never budged a wing, and of the fogs
around Newfoundland, that a sailor
could carve with a knife, or cork in bottles,
and of monstrous whales,
and ice on rigging you could play like bells —
all of the tales

I'd heard in the magic dark
or in gaslight fluttering
from a broken mantle — a sailor's world
he'd lost forever. And now again,
and finally,
he tried to give what wealth he'd gained —
those hints of possibility

that goad young blood, and dissolve the walls
of sick-rooms. Gently we took away
our son, forgotten now
as the old boy muttered, and
left him there
before she came back, with half the neighbourhood
and his nightly beer.

BRIAN JONES

DISCUSSION

1   Read the poem carefully and pick out clues to find out how the old man feels about his present life. Do you think he leads a sad life in comparison to his life as a sailor?

2   The poem seems to change from describing something quite ordinary to something more exciting and magical. Where does this happen and what would the poem lose if the poet had not introduced this new element?

DRAMA

Going home for a visit

Organisation: Read the poem again. Work with a partner. One of you will be Ada, the young wife in the poem, and the other is a friend or relation of hers.

Situation: Ada and her husband and child have been to visit her parents-in-law. Ada describes to her friend what the visit was like and how she felt about it. She asks advice about how to tell her husband that she doesn't want to go there again.

Opening line: ADA: It's really dismal round there.

Relations

Organisation: Work in a small group. One of you is the mother-in-law in the poem 'Bill', and the others in the groups are sympathetic neighbours.

Situation: You have all noticed that Ada and her husband seem uneasy when they visit their in-laws. What is your opinion of Ada and her husband?

Opening line: NEIGHBOUR: Well, that Ada seems a stuck-up piece. We're not good enough for the likes of her.

A Visit to Grandpa's

In the middle of the night I woke from a dream full of whips and
lariats as long as serpents, and runaway coaches on mountain
passes, and wide, windy gallops over cactus fields, and I heard the
man in the next room crying, 'Gee-up!' and 'Whoa!' and trotting his
tongue on the roof of his mouth.

It was the first time I had stayed in grandpa's house. The
floorboards had squeaked like mice as I climbed into bed, and the
mice between the walls had creaked like wood as though another
visitor was walking on them. It was a mild summer night, but
curtains had flapped and branches beaten against the window. I had
pulled the sheets over my head, and soon was roaring and riding in a
book.

'Whoa there, my beauties!' cried grandpa. His voice sounded
very young and loud, and his tongue had powerful hooves, and he
made his bedroom into a great meadow. I thought I would see if he
was ill, or had set his bedclothes on fire, for my mother had said that
he lit his pipe under the blankets, and had warned me to run to his
help if I smelt smoke in the night. I went on tiptoe through the
darkness to his bedroom door, brushing against the furniture and
upsetting a candlestick with a thump. When I saw there was a light
in the room I felt frightened, and as I opened the door I heard
grandpa shout, 'Gee-up!' as loudly as a bull with a megaphone.

He was sitting straight up in bed and rocking from side to side as
though the bed were on a rough road; the knotted edges of the
counterpane were his reins; his invisible horse stood in a shadow
beyond the bedside candle. Over a white flannel nightshirt he was
wearing a red waistcoat with walnut-sized brass buttons. The over-
filled bowl of his pipe smouldered among his whiskers like a little,
burning hayrick on a stick. At the sight of me, his hands dropped
from the reins and lay blue and quiet, the bed stopped still on a level
road, he muffled his tongue into silence, and the horses drew softly
up.

'Is there anything the matter, grandpa?' I asked, though the
clothes were not on fire. His face in the candlelight looked like a
ragged quilt pinned upright on the black air and patched all over
with goat beards.

He stared at me mildly. Then he blew down his pipe, scattering
the sparks and making a high, wet dog-whistle of the stem, and
shouted: 'Ask no questions.'

After a pause, he said slyly: 'Do you ever have nightmares, boy?'

I said: 'No.'

'Oh, yes, you do,' he said.

I said I was woken by a voice that was shouting to horses.

'What did I tell you?' he said. 'You eat too much. Who ever
heard of horses in a bedroom?'

He fumbled under his pillow, brought out a small tinkling bag,
and carefully untied its strings. He put a sovereign in my hand, and
said: 'Buy a cake.' I thanked him and wished him goodnight.

As I closed my bedroom door, I heard his voice crying loudly and
gaily, 'Gee-up! gee-up!' and the rocking of the travelling bed.

from *A Visit to Grandpa's* by Dylan Thomas

*   *   *   *   *

Beside me sat Grandma, combing her hair back from her knitted
brows and muttering to herself. He blue-black hair was remarkable
for its abundance. It came below her knees and even reached the
ground. She had to hold it up with one hand while, with the other,
she drew an almost toothless comb through its heavy mass. The
strain made her lips purse and brought an exaggerated sharpness to
her eyes. There was something almost bitter in her expression; yet,
when I asked why her hair was so long, it was in her usual melodious
words and her customary tender intonations that she answered,
'God must have given it to me to punish me. It's combed out but
look at it! When I was a girl I was proud of that mane, but now I
curse it. But sleep, child. It's early yet. The sun's barely up.'

'I want to get up.'

'Well then, get up' she said.

Her words were like music and like flowers. They bloom in my
memory like everlasting blossoms. I remember her smile as a
dilation of her large eyes and a cheerful flash of her white teeth that
gave her face an inexpressible charm. Despite her wrinkles and her
weathered complexion she looked young and even glowing. All that
spoiled her appearance was her bulbous, red nose with its splayed-
out nostrils, the result of a weakness for drink and her snuff-taking.
Outwardly she looked dark, but within burned a vigorous,
inextinguishable flame of which the radiance in her eyes was a
reflection. She was so stooped as to be almost hunchbacked, yet her
motions were gliding and light like those of a great cat; and she was
soft and caressing like a cat.

from *My Childhood* by Maxim Gorky

DRAMA

The Visit

Organisation: Work with a partner. Both of you are young people, perhaps friends or cousins.

Situation: One of you has recently been on a visit to stay with an elderly friend or relative. (Choose one of the extracts you have read to base your work on.) You are telling your friend what happened during the visit.

Opening line: YOUNG PERSON: I had a great time . . .

WRITING

1 Write a description of an old person you know, putting in all the details you can think of. Remember to describe the old person's personality and habits, as well as their appearance.

2 Write a story which might begin with one of the following lines:
a His only friend was Grandad . . .
b A day out with Gran was terrific. . .
c When I grow up, I'm going to live with you, Gran.

* * * * *

Childhood

I used to think that grown-up people chose
To have stiff backs and wrinkles round their nose,
And veins like small fat snakes on either hand,
On purpose to be grand.
Till through the banisters I watched one day
My great-aunt Effy's friend who was going away,
And how her onyx beads had come unstrung.
I saw her grope to find them as they rolled;
And then I knew that she was helplessly old,
As I was helplessly young.

Frances Cornford

65

Warning

When I am an old woman I shall wear purple
With a red hat which doesn't go, and doesn't suit me,
And I shall spend my pension on brandy and summer gloves
And satin sandals, and say we've no money for butter.
I shall sit down on the pavement when I'm tired
And gobble up samples in shops and press alarm bells
And run my stick along the public railings
And make up for the sobriety of my youth.
I shall go out in my slippers in the rain
And pick the flowers from other people's gardens,
And learn to spit.

You can wear terrible shirts and grow more fat
And eat three pounds of sausages at a go
Or only bread and pickle for a week
And hoard pens and pencils and beermats and things in boxes.

But now we must have clothes that keep us dry
And pay our rent and not swear in the street,
And set a good example for the children.
We will have friends to dinner and read the papers.

But maybe I ought to practise a little now?
So people who know me are not too shocked and surprised
When suddenly I am old and start to wear purple.

Jenny Joseph

DISCUSSION

The first poem conveys a young child's impression of old age.
The child suddenly realises how closely young and old are
linked. In the next poem, the writer is contemplating the kind
of life she would like to lead in her old age.

1   Old age is often referred to as a 'second childhood'. Old
people may have fewer responsibilities; their families have
grown-up and once they have retired they have a lot more time
for themselves. Have you ever noticed that children often get

along much better with older people than with people of their parents' generation? Why should this be? Do people's attitudes, outlook and concerns change with age?

2 *And then I knew that she was helplessly old,*
   As I was helplessly young.
   Can you explain the idea the author is trying to express in this sentence?

3 Write a list of all the things that Jenny Joseph in *Warning* wants to do when she is old. How many of these things have you been tempted to do? Can you think of any other things she might enjoy doing? Can you imagine your parents wanting to do similar things? Do you think Jenny Joseph will have the courage to carry out most of her ambitions?

WRITING

Write a poem or short passage on how you see yourself when you are old. What will you look like? Will you behave like Jenny Joseph? Then compare your work with other people's and decide what 'tone' each of you has adopted in your writing — you might find that some of the poems or passages are humorous in tone while others are more thoughtful or even sad.

YOUR OWN GRANNY PROJECT

Ivan obviously enjoyed talking to his Granny and he was fascinated by her memories. Your grandparents or elderly friends have lifetimes of experience and of history as it was being made.

You could put together information about an elderly person's life and present it in the form of a 'Story of a lifetime' as we have done for Irene Dyer on *page* 70. Photographs as well as tape recordings of some conversations would make your project more interesting. Alternatively you could write up your findings as Michelle McCarthy has done in her piece 'The Olden Days'. In either case you may want to take some of the following suggestions as starting points.

Childhood, with references to school, family life, homes and the environment, holidays, feast days, birthdays, Christmas, local customs, illnesses, games, toys, pranks, punishments.

Work, with descriptions of places of work, daily routines, interesting characters, money earned.

Social Life, looking at dances, sports, cinema, theatre, music, clothes, hairstyles, cars and transport.

Family Matters, including marriages, courtship and weddings, children and parenthood, how the old were cared for then.

Historical Events such as wars, coronations, social changes eg. in housing, health, social services, governments, leaders.

Individual Experiences which are not included above such as hobbies, travels, political and social activities.

THE OLDEN DAYS

My nan was born on January 26th 1920 and lived in Co.
Durham in the north of England. When she was about six,
there was a general strike in this country. When she went to
school at about 11.30 in the morning they assembled in twos
from each classroom and walked about a mile holding each
others' hands until they came to a church.

They used to line up for dinner just like kids do for school
nowadays. After, when they had had something to eat, they
went back to school exactly the same way to finish their work.

They never had a lot of money in those days and nearly
everybody claimed the dole which is equal to the Social
Security now, and they never had any family allowances
either. They used to wear ordinary clothes for school and keep
their best clothes for Sunday. Food was a lot cheaper then.
Papers they read were cheaper so were cigarettes and sweets.

Schooling was the same then as it is now. They used to be in
class at 9.15 in the morning until 3.30 in the afternoon and
when they went into the Juniors, they finished school at 4
o'clock in the afternoon. They used to do the same lessons as
today, but didn't do any foreign languages like French or
German.

When she was fourteen and a half years, she left Co. Durham
and came to London and had to leave her family as there
wasn't much work up north. She started working in large
buildings and her wages were 10/- which is about 50p
nowadays. They woke up at 5 o'clock in the morning, had a
quick cup of tea, started work at 5.30 until 8.30. Breakfast was
at 9 o'clock then they had to work until 12 o'clock mid-day.
They had one hour lunch break then back to work until 3
o'clock and had the rest of the afternoon off. She worked in
large buildings in Piccadilly doing guest bedrooms, corridors
and bathrooms.

When the war was on she worked in Wembley Stadium in a
factory. She said that she enjoyed her life but it was hard work
and if she finished a job she had to find another one straight
away for the next day as she had nowhere to go and no
relations in London to look after her.

She enjoyed her life, all the same.

Michelle McCarthy, Stockwell Park School

Studio portrait taken when Irene was three. 'It was all frills and ribbons and little black boots in those days.'

Irene at 17. The photograph was taken at Emberson's studio at Tooting Junction. 'It was a fad to have your picture taken!'

Irene and her mother in the pub in the late 1950s. 'I had a wonderful mother. She taught me a lot. She was a born nurse. If anyone was ill in our road, they'd come along to my mother, and she'd say if they needed to go to the doctor.'

On honeymoon with Frank at Southsea, 1935. 'We only had a week's holiday. It seemed a lot then.'

Irene today. 'I've had a hectic life one way or another.'

Story of a lifetime

Irene Dyer: Important dates in her life	Important dates in the 20th century
	1901 Queen Victoria dies.
	1903 First powered flight by Wright Brothers in USA.
	1906 Free school dinners introduced.
	1908 Old Age Pension introduced.
27 January 1909 Irene Ethel Jackson born, Mitcham, Surrey.	
	1914 First World War begins.
	1918 First World War ends. Women over age of 30 first given right to vote. Education Act raises school leaving age to 14.
Irene leaves Links 1923 Road School and gets her first job in Mitcham.	
	1926 General Strike.
	1929 Stock market crash in USA. Depression spreads to Britain.
Irene marries Frank 1935 Dyer	
Irene and Frank's 1939 daughter, Delia, born.	Second World War begins.
Frank killed in 1944 action, Caen, France.	
	1945 Second World War ends; Labour Government elected.
Irene returns to 1946 work at Renshaw's Confectionery factory, Mitcham.	Socialist legislation (National Health Service Bill, etc.)
	1953 Coronation of Elizabeth II.
	1956 Suez Crisis.
Irene's daughter, 1959 Delia, marries.	
	1963 The Swinging 60s, (miniskirts, the Beatles, Carnaby Street, etc.)
Irene retires from 1969 Renshaw's.	Man lands on the moon.
	1973 Britain enters Common Market.
	1979 Margaret Thatcher, first woman Prime Minister of Britain.
	1982 Argentinian occupation of the Falklands Islands ended by UK Task Force.
Irene visits Frank's 1984 grave in France.	Miners' strike in Britain.

The following poem was written by an elderly lady in hospital.

A CRABBIT OLD WOMAN

What do you see nurses, what do you see?
Are you thinking when you are looking at me —
A crabbit old woman, not very wise,
Uncertain of habit, with faraway eyes,
Who dribbles her food and makes no reply
When you say in a loud voice — 'I do wish you'd try.'
Who seems not to notice the things that you do,
And forever is losing a stocking or shoe.
Who unresisting or not, lets you do as you will,
With bathing and feeding, the long day to fill.
Is that what you are thinking, is that what you see?
Then open your eyes, nurse, you are looking at me.
I'll tell you who I am as I sit here so still;
As I use at your bidding, as I eat at your will,
I'm a small child of ten with a father and mother,
Brothers and sisters who love one another.
A young girl of sixteen with wings on her feet,
Dreaming that soon now a lover she'll meet;
A bride soon at twenty — my heart gives a leap,
Remembering the vows that I promised to keep;
At twenty-five now I have young of my own,
Who need me to build a secure, happy home;
A woman of thirty, my young now grown fast,
Bound to each other with ties that should last;
At forty, my young sons now grow and will be gone,
At fifty once more babies play round my knee,
Again we know children, my loved one and me,
Dark days are upon me, my husband is dead,
I look at the future, I shudder with dread
For my young are all busy rearing young of their own,
I'm an old woman now and nature is cruel —
'Tis her jest to make old age look like a fool.
The body it crumbles, grace and vigour depart.
There is now a stone where I once had a heart;
But inside this old carcass a young girl still dwells
And now and again my battered heart swells,
I remember the joys, I remember the pain
And I'm loving and living life all over again.
I think of the years all too few — gone too fast
And accept the stark fact that nothing can last.
So open your eyes, nurses, open and see
Not a crabbit old woman, look closer — see ME!

DRAMA

Stages in a life

Organisation: Work in a group of three or four. Look carefully at 'Story of a Lifetime' and 'A Crabbit Old Woman', and choose one of these to work on.

Situation: Devise a series of tableaux or 'still pictures', which show the key moments in the different stages of the person's life. Use as many or as few of the group as you need for each picture.

Give each of your 'pictures' a title.

Development: Each character in your 'pictures' could speak their thoughts, which will vary with the moment which is being represented. Perhaps each one could make clear what is their greatest concern. What worries do they have? What are their hopes for the future?

Remembering events

Organisation: Work in pairs. One of you is a reporter for a local newspaper. The other is one of the elderly people from the extracts and poem you have read. Choose carefully which old person you want to be.

Situation: The reporter has come to interview the old person for an article which is being written in the local paper. The old person may be getting rather forgetful, but the reporter has done a good deal of research, and knows how to help the old person to recall important moments in their life.

Opening line: REPORTER: Good evening. I'm from *The Gazette* . . .

WRITING

1 Imagine that you are the old lady in 'A Crabbit Old Woman' and that you keep a diary. Write an entry in your diary for *four* stages of your life, the last entry being the one you write in hospital.

2 Write the article which might arise from the interview with the reporter.

OLD AGE IN BRITAIN TODAY

How many elderly people?

In 1981, the Census showed that 7 985 102 elderly people were living in Britain. More detailed statistics are as follows:

Age	Total population	Men	Women
65-74	4 932 307	43.8%	56.2%
75–84	2 500 408	34.6	65.4
85–94	521 786	23.8	76.2
95+	30 601	17.9	82.1

		Men	Women
Married	Single	8.0%	12.1%
or	Married	73.0	37.2
single	Widowed	17.4	48.9
(65 and over)	Divorced	1.6	1.8

Source: 1981 Census

These two tables show important differences between elderly men and women. Fewer men reach 65, and most of those that do, die sooner than women. Most elderly men are married: just over 1 in 4 is not. In contrast, almost 2 out of every 3 women are either widowed or divorced, or have never married.

The human face of these statistics is often sad. Many elderly women are on their own, either because they have never married or because their husbands have died. The older they are, the more likely they are to have to cope alone. Over 90 per cent of women aged 85 to 89, for instance, are single or widowed.

A lonely old age

This table shows the percentage of elderly people (65 and over) living with others or on their own.

	Men %	Women %
With husband or wife only	63	34
With husband or wife and other people	10	4
Without husband or wife but with other people*	7	16
Alone	20	45

* Other people includes children, brothers or sisters, relatives or friends
Source: General Household Survey 1983

How much money do they have?

The short answer is: not very much. The table below shows how much income elderly households have. The term 'household' means a home, no matter what sort of building it is or how many people it contains. An 'elderly household' is one in which the head of the household is over 65. Bear in mind that the average industrial wage for an individual worker in 1981 was £116.80 per week. The statistics are from the 1981 Census.

Weekly income	Elderly household average (1.7 people)	Non-elderly household average (3.1 people)
Under £55	40.4%	5.7%
£55 and under £120	41.1	20.1
£120 and under £200	11.9	33.8
£200 and above	6.6	40.4

How is it spent?

The next table compares how elderly and non-elderly households spend their money each week. The statistics are for 1981.

These figures show that elderly people spend far more of their income on basic necessities such as fuel, housing and food. If the cost of these 'basics' increases, most wage-earning families can cope, even if they have to cut spending on other, less important, things. Elderly people do not find this so easy. If electricity prices rise, or their rent, or basic foods, they face real difficulties. For some old people, winter brings a choice between eating a good meal or keeping warm. Compare this pattern of spending with your family's.

	Elderly household	Non-elderly household
Fuel, light and power	£ 6.25	£ 7.88
Housing	15.56	21.20
Food	17.03	30.69
Services	8.47	15.69
'Other' goods	4.73	11.06
Tobacco	1.80	4.40
Alcoholic drink	2.68	7.21
Clothing and footwear	3.99	11.02
Transport and vehicles	7.27	22.61
Durable household goods	3.44	11.43
Miscellaneous	0.21	0.71
Total	£71.43	£143.90

WRITING

1   Using only the statistics provided, write an article for your local paper entitled: 'Old Age in Britain Today'.

2   Consider the disadvantages of retiring to the coast all year round. An elderly friend has written asking your advice about a move to the coast. Write a reply to your friend, persuading him or her not to retire to the coast.

AMENITIES IN YOUR AREA

1   Make a list of all the local amenities you use and how long it takes to reach them. What mode of transport do you use?

2   Draw an amenity index with your house at the centre, showing modes of transport used to reach each one.

3   Imagine you are now over 60. Write a list of the amenities you need: Library, Post Office (for pension), Hospital. Put down the time it takes to reach them on foot or by bus. Plot an amenity index using your house as a centre, bearing in mind that most elderly people travel on foot or by bus.

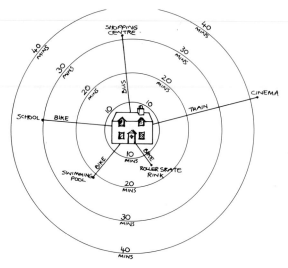

4 Imagine you have the job of designing a new housing development in the country with old people in mind. Consider their needs and draw the plan for your development.

ENTERTAINING THE ELDERLY

1 Make a class newspaper aimed at the elderly.

2 Tape a radio programme designed for elderly listeners.

3 Organise a weekend away for 20 elderly people. They are all mobile and enjoy outside as well as indoor activities. Make a timetable for your weekend, offering a choice of activities wherever possible.

4 Write a page for a travel brochure aimed at elderly travellers. Comment on the sight-seeing, guided tours and entertainments available.

5 Imagine that you are a social worker compiling a pamphlet entitled 'Adopt a Granny' which is aimed at secondary school students. Design an attractive cover and layout for the pamphlet.
Write the pamphlet including advice on the services a student might offer, explaining how both will benefit from the visits and gently warning the students of problems they may face.